Never Tell A Lie

Fake Billionaire Series, Volume 4

Lexy Timms

Published by Dark Shadow Publishing, 2017.

NEVER TELL A LIE

First edition. December 2, 2017.

Written by Lexy Timms.

Also by Lexy Timms

Making the Break

Conquering Warrior Series
Ruthless

Diamond in the Rough Anthology
Billionaire Rock
Billionaire Rock - part 2

Dominating PA Series
Her Personal Assistant - Part 1
Her Personal Assistant Box Set

Fake Billionaire Series
Faking It
Temporary CEO
Caught in the Act
Never Tell A Lie

Firehouse Romance Series
Caught in Flames
Burning With Desire
Craving the Heat
Firehouse Romance Complete Collection

Celtic Rune
Celtic Mann
Heart of the Battle Series Box Set

Just About Series
About Love

Justice Series
Seeking Justice
Finding Justice
Chasing Justice
Pursuing Justice
Justice - Complete Series

Love You Series
Love Life
Need Love
My Love

Managing the Bosses Series
The Boss
The Boss Too
Who's the Boss Now
Love the Boss
I Do the Boss
Wife to the Boss

Employed by the Boss
Brother to the Boss
Senior Advisor to the Boss
Forever the Boss
Gift for the Boss - Novella 3.5
Christmas With the Boss

Moment in Time
Highlander's Bride
Victorian Bride
Modern Day Bride
A Royal Bride
Forever the Bride

Outside the Octagon
Submit

RIP Series
Track the Ripper
Hunt the Ripper
Pursue the Ripper

R&S Rich and Single Series
Alex Reid
Parker

Whisky Harmony

The Debt
The Debt: Part 1 - Damn Horse
The Debt: Complete Collection

The University of Gatica Series
The Recruiting Trip
Faster
Higher
Stronger
Dominate
No Rush
University of Gatica - The Complete Series

T.N.T. Series
Troubled Nate Thomas - Part 1
Troubled Nate Thomas - Part 2
Troubled Nate Thomas - Part 3

Undercover Series
Perfect For Me
Perfect For You
Perfect For Us

Never
TELL A LIE

Fake BILLIONAIRE SERIES

USA TODAY BESTSELLING AUTHOR
LEXY TIMMS

Never Tell A Lie
Fake Billionaire Series # 4

Copyright 2017 by Lexy Timms
Cover by: Book Cover by Design[1]

Never Tell a Lie Blurb

"Hurt me with the truth, don't ever comfort me with a lie..."
Newly married in a spur-of-the-moment Bahama wedding, Allyson Smith is trying to figure out how to manage working with her billionaire husband, Dane Prescott. Wait, it's Allyson Prescott now. She's no longer his assistant, and she's now insanely rich. That's going to take some adjusting to.

Weary of her family's money-hungry ways, and Dane's untrusting family, Allyson makes every effort to tread carefully. However, you can't please everyone all the time and eventually something has to give. Or someone gets caught with their hand in the cookie jar.

When Allyson's accused of embezzling, Dane is willing to take the fall—and prison term—for his wife. Can their marriage survive this attack, or will the lies continue to pile up and swallow them whole?

Fake Billionaire Series

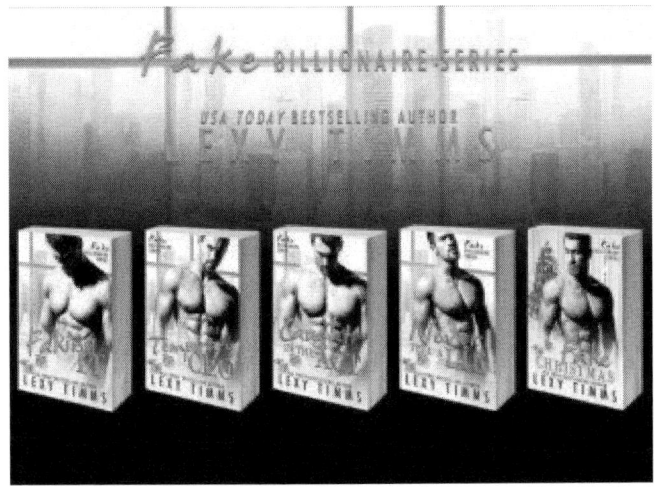

Faking It
Book 1
Temporary CEO
Book 2
Caught in the Act
Book 3
Never Tell a Lie
Book 4
Fake Christmas
Book 5 Novella

Find Lexy Timms

Lexy Timms Newsletter:
http://eepurl.com/9i0vD
Lexy Timms Facebook Page:
https://www.facebook.com/SavingForever
Lexy Timms Website:
http://www.lexytimms.com

Want to read more...
For **FREE?**
Sign up for Lexy Timms' newsletter
And she'll send you
A paid read, for FREE!
Sign up for news and updates!
http://eepurl.com/9i0vD

Chapter 1

"I bet you this place is haunted."

Dane Prescott glanced at his beautiful wife and laughed. "No way. Don't tell me you believe in ghosts."

"I mean, look at it." Allyson motioned to the stately townhouse before them. "It looks like it was built in the eighteenth century."

She shivered, and he wrapped his arm around her, pulling her close. No doubt the chilly autumn air was getting through her cashmere coat, but maybe she was shivering because the old house really had spooked her. "Do you still want to go inside?" he asked.

Biting her lower lip she nodded, resolve on her lovely face. "Totally. I want to see why this house is worth six million dollars."

With his arm still around her he guided her up the walkway, then up the step to the front porch. Allyson reached up to ring the doorbell and they waited. "We ring, right? You don't just walk in to view a place like this?" She shifted her weight, rocking slightly.

The house was a little old-fashioned for his taste with its colonial style, front porch columns, and brick façade. Still, finding a gated community like this in New York City had been one of Allyson's lucky finds. In the months they'd spent house-hunting, this place seemed to be the only one that met all of his wife's requirements. At least on paper anyway.

Suddenly, the front door swung open and their real estate agent, Nancy Sanchez, stepped out to greet them. As always, she was perfectly dressed—Dane would say probably overdressed—from the top of her swept- up hair to the genuine pearl bracelet she always wore. Dane had been wealthy long enough to know that the bracelet was the real thing, not costume jewelry.

Nancy grinned at them, her smile so wide that it made her eyes crinkle. The same smile that was reserved for her most exclusive clients. The sort of smile that would be frozen on her face all day. A smile that was only reserved for people like the Prescotts. "It's so wonderful to see you two," Nancy said excitedly. "You're going to *love* this place—I just know it!"

She ushered them inside.

As they stepped into the house Allyson gasped, her green eyes sparkling. "Oh, Dane, look. It's just perfect."

He furrowed his eyebrows. The interior was more modern than the exterior would have suggested, but he didn't share his wife's excitement. "Let's see the whole house first," he cautioned.

From their vantage point he could already see that a large part of the ground floor was open concept, which allowed the natural light from outside to fill up the space.

But something gnawed at him. The same unease he had felt for the last few months while they had been house-hunting. He and Allyson had been married for six months. They had been the happiest six months of his life. She filled his life with more happiness than he could have ever imagined. Honestly, some days he thought it must be a crime to be as happy as he was.

And yet, the uneasy feeling remained. Like wearing shoes that were just a little bit too small. It wasn't the marriage. It was the fact that they had been searching for houses that were relatively close to Prescott Global. So many of their decisions revolved around what Prescott Global needed.

After they had wrenched control back from the double-crossing Handel siblings nearly six months ago, Dane had agreed to stay on as CEO. He'd signed a six-month contract, because he wasn't sure if he wanted to stay on. Yes, it was his family's company. Yes, he wanted it to succeed. Yes, before Allison, it had been the most important thing in the world to him. And it still was important. Of course it was. However, it was just...

He expected he'd renew the contract soon now that the six months was almost up, and that had been the cause of his unease. He would sign the contract renewal, but he had no idea why he was doing it. The fire in the belly he'd once had running the company simply wasn't there. Not that he'd told Allyson that. Her happiness was far too important for him to reveal that he was grappling with something he really shouldn't have been grappling with. Especially after she had gone to such lengths to save the company from ruin in the first place.

"I love the hardwood floors." Allyson laced her arm around his, her face lighting up. The autumn chill had stained her cheeks a beautiful shade of pink. She had grown her black hair out, and there had been many nights when Dane had run his hands through the silky waves after their lovemaking.

He couldn't help smiling to himself. That part of their marriage hadn't changed in six months. They still had a hard time keeping their hands to themselves. But that didn't surprise him. His wife was so tempting and sexy, he really couldn't imagine keeping his hands off her.

Leaning towards her, he planted a kiss on the corner of her sensuous mouth. The blush in her cheeks deepened and she smiled at him. Every smile he managed to coax from her felt like a reward. A reward he could never get tired of. Never get enough of.

The real estate agent started to give them a tour, leading them around the ground floor. Dane was surprised to discover how ultra-modern the kitchen was. It was complete with state-of-the-art technology.

"You can program the stove, oven, and refrigerator from just about anywhere in the house," Nancy explained as she gestured around the kitchen. "Even the grill outside is programmable. As is the fireplace in the living room and the fire pit outside. The security system is also part of the smart tech that comes with the house. You can even hook up the security system to be programmed from your car if you want."

Allyson's eyes widened. "I guess we've figured out why this house is worth what it is."

"Are you still afraid of the ghosts?" he asked, lowering his voice to whisper in her ear.

"Not if you're with me." Her sultry voice was already driving him crazy with desire for her. She wrapped her arms around his torso and arched her back, her lips finding his.

Before he could return the kiss, the sound of Nancy softly clearing her throat made him pause. He broke the kiss and exchanged a sheepish grin with his wife.

"Sorry," Allyson said, pulling away from him.

Nancy waved her hand. "That's quite all right. I know how you newlyweds can be." The agent motioned for them to follow her out of the kitchen.

When they finally finished the tour of the house interior, Nancy led them outside.

"I'm going to make a call to the owner to let them know you two have seen the property," Nancy said, taking her cell phone out of her pocket. "You guys can talk and view the property if you'd like while I'm on the phone." Nancy stepped back into the house, leaving Dane and Allyson outside on the back porch.

They sat down side by side on the patio swing that overlooked the backyard.

Allyson let out a contented sigh, and snuggled up to him. Wrapping his arm around her shoulder he held her close, enjoying the sensation of her warm, soft body against his. There really was nothing better than spending a Sunday afternoon with the woman he loved.

"I can just imagine us having dinner parties here," she said. "We could invite all our new friends."

He frowned at that. It should have made him happy that his wife was excited about the prospect of entertaining guests, but Dane wasn't exactly a fan of Allyson's new friends. They were from the upper class. Mostly business types they had met through his mother.

Like the rest of New York's high society, they had taken to Allyson after she saved Prescott Global from ruin. But Allyson wasn't used to the fickle nature of high society. One day you were up, the next you were down. Loyalty and genuine friendship weren't common among people like that. The relationships that New York's wealthy cultivated were almost always based on what they could get out of it. Friendships and marriages were a mercenary venture as people clawed their way to the top. Dane had long suspected that Allyson was their new target. She was beautiful, and had saved the Prescott fortune from the Handels. Not to mention, for weeks after Prescott Global had been saved he and his wife had been the talk of all the local gossip rags. To her surprise and delight high society had flocked to her, but he sensed that Allyson would only end up disappointed.

She sat up to face him. "I know you're skeptical of them, but if you gave them a chance—"

"I have given them a chance," he pointed out. "I invited some of your friends to the awards ceremony next week." He wasn't one for awards and accolades, but the local business community was giving him an award for all of his work at Prescott over the past year. Truth be told, Allyson was probably more excited about it than he was.

"That's for work," she murmured. "I really want you to get to know them outside of work."

"I've been surrounded by people like that my whole life," he said. "There's a reason I only have a handful of friends, Allyson." The truth was, he didn't trust Allyson's new friends. He was suspicious of their motives, and he wouldn't be surprised if they took advantage of his wife's trusting nature and knifed her in the back.

"Yes, but isn't it a good thing that I'm making friends?" she asked. "It's better than having high society shut me out like we thought they would."

"Some members of high society are so bad, being shut out is a blessing compared to being friends with them." The atmosphere around them had suddenly grown tense in the wake of their disagreement.

She turned to face the yard, the expression on her face souring. Trying to convince her to see things his way seemed to be backfiring already. The more he tried to warn her, the more she would dig in her heels. Which meant she'd head right towards the very people most likely to do her harm. "You don't like the house either, do you?"

"It's not that I don't like it," he said. "The outside is old-fashioned."

She tilted her head, her suspicious gaze falling on him. "That's it? That's the only reason?"

How to tell her about his apprehension? The apprehension he felt about making such huge decisions based on what was good for Prescott Global, rather than what was right for them.

Her huge green eyes were curious. As if she were asking him a tender question with her eyes alone. As if she could sense the unease that had roiled through him these past few months.

He weighed whether to unburden himself and tell her. Shook that thought from his mind. No. Allyson loved working at Prescott Global. She was now part of the team that was building the women's division from the ground up. Over the past six months she had not only worked at a top position at Prescott, she had also enrolled in a university business program. Most of her classes took place at night or were online, and she was so dedicated. She had put in so much work. How could he tell her that the company that was making her so happy and fulfilled now felt like a noose tightening around his neck?

"I'll miss the view at our apartment," he finally said. "Looking out over the balcony at the city...especially at night. It's like having New York City in the palm of your hand."

"Our apartment does have a nice view." She smiled. "But I love the feeling this place gives me. It's like having a little bit of the country in the city." She looked back at the yard, her entire body seeming to relax.

The leaves on the trees surrounding the yard had all changed. The autumn foliage really was spectacular, having turned into remarkable shades of red and gold.

And yet, the view from their luxury apartment was unparalleled. There might be good technology in this house, but the inside didn't strike him as being like the ultramodern interior of their luxury apartment.

"I don't want to rush you into anything," she continued.

He glanced at her, wondering what on earth he had done to deserve a woman like her. It was obvious that this was the house of her dreams. The house she had been longing for. But here she was, still ready to risk losing it for his sake.

Finally he said, "Let's talk about it some more. Weigh our options."

She nodded, then chewed her lip. "You won't object to me inviting my friends when we do settle on a house, will you?"

"Of course not. Why would I object?"

"Well...you don't like them," she reminded him.

Dane wrapped his arm around her again. "That doesn't mean you can't invite them."

"I know," she said. "I just feel like my friends are pulling away a bit. It would be nice for everyone to get together and bond over a house-warming party."

He didn't say anything. Just leaned forward to plant a kiss on the top of her head. It wouldn't help her to reveal what he was really thinking deep down. Deep down, he suspected her high society friends were pulling away not because Allyson had middle-class beginnings, but because she now had more wealth than she knew what to do with. Getting a house like this meant that Allyson was moving ahead in the world.

And if there was one thing the upper class hated more than no money, it was someone like Allyson having a lot of it.

As he held on to her tightly he couldn't bear to tell the woman he loved that maybe the worst thing Allyson could do wasn't to fail, but to succeed.

Chapter 2

Allyson Prescott now had a love-hate relationship with Mondays. With a cup of coffee in one hand, she stepped inside the elevator. The hate part was easy to identify for a Monday. As usual for a Monday morning, the elevator was crowded. Monday mornings were her early mornings when she met with the women's division support staff to prepare for the week. This morning was already especially grueling because she had woken up even earlier when her husband got out of bed at five o'clock.

As the elevator went up to the fiftieth floor, she smiled to herself. Working with Dane was the best part of her job at Prescott Global. It was so wonderful to see his face every day. Hear his voice. No matter how hectic things got at work, just having him around made her day better. Not many people could say they loved working with their spouses. They were the exception to the rule.

When the elevator finally stopped at the fiftieth floor she stepped out, making her way to her office. There was so much she had to get through today. For one thing, there was that final interview she was going to have to deal with.

Reaching for the printout on her desk, she quickly scanned the list of names. Today was the day she'd be interviewing the last candidate for the position of her own assistant. It seemed surreal. After six months of working at Prescott Global, it was time to buckle down and make a choice. Using the executive assistants was running them ragged. She'd been Dane's assistant and knew what it required. That's why the decision was so hard. She needed someone willing to work as hard as she had. Someone who—

A knock at her door caught her attention. She smiled when her husband opened the door.

"Good morning, handsome." She winked. "Sorry... good morning, Mr. Prescott."

He leaned forward, his impossibly tall frame taking up the entire doorway. The smile on his face made her heart flutter wildly. He still made her giddy. Right now he looked absolutely delicious in the navy-blue suit that fit his hard, muscular body perfectly. "Hello, Mrs. Prescott. Or can I just call you 'Sexy'?"

"I believe that borders on sexual harassment, Mr. CEO."

He held his hands out. "What's my punishment?"

She winked. "I'll figure that out when we get home." She realized her office door was still open and she cleared her throat. If they hadn't been at work, she would've raced into his arms and kissed him, coming up with some kind of naught-but-nice punishment. But they *were* at work, so she reminded herself that they needed to be on their best behavior. She straightened and cleared her throat. "How was your meeting with the investors?"

"Boring." There was a glint in his blue eyes, as if the meeting had been anything but boring.

She raised an eyebrow. "What are you up to?"

He shrugged. "Nothing. Why do I have to be up to something?"

"I know you, Dane," she said. "And you're up to something." Setting her coffee cup down on her desk, she turned complete focus onto her husband. She motioned to the door and then beckoned to him, the sudden urge to have him close overpowering. Screw being professional, she'd rather screw him.

Dane turned and shut the door, grinning like a Cheshire cat, then sauntered over to her. He wrapped his big, strong arms around her waist. His touch was bold. Possessive. The heat of it practically melting her.

Knowing it was more than a little scandalous to take things further with her husband at work, but eager for more, she pressed her lips to his. He groaned.

"Allyson... I didn't lock the door."

"Makes it... a bit... more... exciting," she mumbled between kisses. She ran her hand down the inside of his jacket and paused on his belt.

He groaned again. "Damn, woman."

Before she could deepen the kiss and slide her hand anywhere else, he suddenly pulled away. Panting slightly Dane held up a key chain, two keys attached to it.

She frowned, disappointed that he seemed to want to keep things professional. "Keys?"

"You have to promise not to get angry."

"I'm not promising anything like that." Her eyes locked on his, defiance surging through her.

"Pity," he said. "I'd hate to incur my wife's wrath at work."

Allyson moved to the side and crossed her arms. She could feel the flush on her cheeks. She'd been teasing him, but she was clearly the one more flustered. "I knew you were up to something! What is it?"

"You really haven't figured it out?" He grinned like a mischievous schoolboy. "It's got four bedrooms, five bathrooms—"

"The house!" Her arms flailed. She was actually flailing. "You didn't!"

"I bought the house," he said. "That's why I left the apartment early. I had to deal with all the paperwork—"

She threw her arms around his shoulders to hug him tightly. "I can't believe you bought the house!" She rained kisses all over his face.

Dane laughed. "I take it you're happy then?"

Happy? She was overjoyed. Finally, she stepped back from him, her heart racing. When she had first seen the listing for the house online, she had been intrigued. Sure, it seemed overpriced, and a little spooky and old- fashioned on the outside, but she knew the interior had potential. One look at the inside of the house yesterday afternoon, and her heart had been set on the place. She had known it was her dream house.

It wasn't just going to be the place she and Dane lived together. This house was going to be a home. Their home. For the first time in her life she had a place that was really hers. And she was going to be living with her husband. Forever.

"When do we start moving in?" she asked breathlessly.

"This week if you like," he said. "By the way, I talked the owner down to five million."

She laughed softly. "Of course you did." Her husband could negotiate anything. When he wanted something, he got it.

Another knock on the door dragged her from her thoughts. Guess sex at work was better left at home. "Come in," she called.

A dark-haired man in glasses stuck his head in. He smiled, his handsome tanned face brightening. He was model good-looking. The kind of guy built for a business suit, and the confidence to catch people's attention. "Good morning. Mr. Prescott, I presume?"

With narrowed eyes, Dane appraised the man. "Yes. And *Mrs.* Prescott. Who the devil are you?"

Allyson glanced at Dane. Was he seriously stressing the Mrs. part? She smiled. Did she detect a hint of jealousy in her husband? Just because a handsome guy was knocking on her office door?

"I'm Cameron. Cameron Bentley." The young man stepped into the room and reached out to shake Allyson's hand. "I'm here for the interview." Cameron was almost as tall as Dane, with wavy brown hair, piercing gray eyes, and a square jaw. His grip was strong, confident. She liked that.

Cameron released her hand to shake Dane's. "It's an honor to meet you both."

"I'm sure," Dane muttered, his tone right on the edge of caustic.

"The way you both took back control of Prescott after the crisis six months ago..." Cameron ended the handshake to adjust his glasses. "It was amazing. The stuff of legend. Everyone's still talking about it."

"Everyone?" Allyson prompted.

"Corporate New Yorkers," Cameron said. "Bankers, CEOs, Wall Street types. It's a fascinating topic during lunch breaks. All in a good way, of course."

"Bluebloods with too much time on their hands," Dane said dismissively. He turned to press a kiss to her cheek and headed for the door. "Good luck with your interview, Bentley."

As she watched her husband stride out of her office, she frowned. Cameron was either too polite or too oblivious to notice that Dane didn't seem to like him much. Her husband had reacted in the same derisive way he had yesterday when she had brought up her friends. In fact, there had been a dark cloud over him when they toured the house. It was like he didn't want to be there. Which is why it was such a surprise to discover that he had impulsively bought the place.

Now that she was replaying yesterday in her mind, an awful sinking feeling started to weigh on her. Dane hadn't been as excited about the house as she had been. Clearly, he had only bought the place to make her happy. At the cost of his own happiness.

In the months since getting Prescott Global back, things had gone so well. The company was thriving under Dane's steady leadership. Just like she knew it would. His contract was going to expire soon but, surely, he would agree to renew it?

A nagging feeling took hold. Yesterday, she had gotten the sneaking suspicion that Dane's hesitation over the house ran deeper than how old the outside looked. He hadn't revealed anything much to her, but sometimes her husband could be hard-headed. Stubborn. Unwilling to relinquish control. Men like Dane didn't give up their secrets easily.

Oh, shit. What if that was it? Was Dane keeping something from her?

"Mrs. Prescott?" Cameron's voice brought her back down to earth.

"Sorry." She motioned for him to sit before taking a seat at her desk.

After Cameron settled down in the seat across from her, he opened the huge binder he had been holding. Quickly, he whipped out some printouts and set them on her desk. "I've included several references with my resume."

"You only needed to bring one reference," she said, glancing at his resume to refresh her memory.

"Can't be too prepared," he said with a smile.

She forced herself to return his smile. Despite the turmoil raging within her, she wanted to put Cameron at ease during his interview. It wouldn't be fair to let her newfound fears about her marriage interfere with work.

Taking a deep breath, Allyson started asking Cameron questions about his education and experience. She focused intently, shoving aside her rising anxiety. They chatted like they knew each other, almost finishing a few of each other's sentences, and when she suggested some work scenarios she was happy to see him respond in a way that she would have working under Dane.

When the interview was over, she smiled at Cameron. He had given an impressive interview, and she thought they might get along well. Like her, he came from a middle-class background, but he had also worked at some high-profile financial firms. Though he seemed a little overeager, he was professional and smart.

"I'd like to hire you, Cameron," she said suddenly.

His gray eyes widened. "Really? That's great." He pushed up his glasses. "When would you like me to start?"

She was taking a chance here, but something about him had her thinking this could work. Her gut was telling her not to miss the opportunity. "Tomorrow," she said. "I'll draw up a contract for you, so you can go over it tonight and bring it in tomorrow."

"Thank you," he said earnestly. "Thank you so much. I can't wait. You won't be disappointed."

After going over some basics, Allyson escorted him out. Then, she settled down to start checking her email.

Dane hadn't liked him but Cameron was supposed to be her assistant, not his. This was a major decision, and over the last six months she had started to learn how to be more independent. Take the initiative and not wait for approval. The work she was doing with the women's division meant so much to her. She knew that her work at Prescott Global was making a difference, and for the first time in her life she felt like she was making real accomplishments. Accomplishments her family might finally be proud of.

Still, a question burned in her mind. Allyson got up and stepped out of her office. Dane's office was right across the hall, so talking to him was always easy. She liked how close his office was.

With a knock on his door, she stepped inside his office.

"How did the interview go?" Dane looked up from his laptop.

"I hired him," she replied.

"I'm shocked," her husband muttered.

She raised an eyebrow. "I detect a hint of sarcasm in your voice."

Her husband's wore a smug expression. "Really?"

"Why don't you like Cameron?" She eased into a chair across from her husband's desk.

"The same reason you seem to like him so much," her husband said. "He's not a bad-looking guy."

She practically choked with laughter. "Cameron? Good-looking?"

"Oh, come on. You know he's handsome," Dane grumbled. "If I can see it, you have to see it."

Truth be told, she hadn't noticed. She had been much more focused on making sure Cameron was the right person for the job. Sure, now that she thought about it she recalled his warm gray eyes, easy smile, and square jaw, but Cameron had other qualities as well. "You honestly think I hired him for his looks?"

"He was the only male candidate," Dane pointed out.

"No, he wasn't," she countered. "There was the guy your mother suggested. The one who dropped out of Harvard."

"And what did he look like?"

She cringed. The Harvard guy hadn't exactly been a looker. "That's not fair."

"Why not?" he asked. "I know how easy it is to fall for your assistant."

With a roll of her eyes she said, "And we all remember how long it took you to actually do something about it."

"Fine," Dane said. "Keep your pretty boy."

Allyson rose to her feet, crossed the room, and without warning sat down in her husband's lap. "I only have eyes for my husband, Mr. Prescott."

He gave her a hard stare, as if trying to admonish her with just one look. "What if someone were to walk in and catch you sitting in the boss' lap?"

She shrugged. "Perks of the job."

The hard expression on his face disappeared, and he started laughing. "I'm going to have to discipline you for insubordination."

"You wouldn't dare," she said with an exaggerated gasp.

Dane locked his arms around her waist and gazed at her. His kissable mouth was mere inches from hers. Angling her head, she covered his lips with hers. He swirled his tongue into her mouth, tasting her expertly. She let out a muffled moan as her tongue entwined with his.

The place between her thighs throbbed. Her entire body was on fire, aching to be touched.

With a groan, Dane suddenly tore his mouth away. Her husband was breathing as heavily as she was. "Allyson, you're going to get me into a lot of trouble."

"You usually like trouble." She started fiddling with the buttons of her blouse.

His huge hands covered hers. "Not at work."

It took every ounce of her strength not to pout, but of course he was right. Working with her husband made her so giddy that sometimes she couldn't think straight. In fact, for the last six months she had been so happy and so blissfully in love that she was terrified. Terrified that the other shoe might drop, and her happiness would blow up in her face. She had never been an overly-pessimistic person, but after the roller coaster with the Handels she really was surprised that disaster hadn't struck again.

And with Dane buying a house that his heart didn't seem set on, fear rippled through her. He was keeping something from her. It hurt her to know that he didn't trust her enough to confide in her. Or maybe his secret was so terrible, confiding in her would destroy their happiness.

Her chest tightened, and her heart began to race. Now was the time to get the truth out of him. "Dane...are you happy about the house?"

Surprise flashed in his eyes. "I'm happy if you're happy. Why?"

"Yesterday, while we were touring the house, you seemed... a little distant."

"You're reading too much into that." His body stiffened. "There's nothing to worry about."

But she was worried. Getting up from his lap, she stood up and stared at him. "Something's wrong. I can sense it. Why won't you tell me what's really been bothering you?"

Chapter 3

He didn't want to talk about it with his wife. Not now. And he sure as hell didn't want to talk about it at work.

With an exasperated sigh, Dane crossed his arms. "We're not doing this right now."

"So something *is* going on." His wife swallowed hard. Shut her eyes as if trying to steel herself. "Just tell me. We can only deal with our problems if you tell me the truth."

Before he could say anything to try to ease her fear his office door opened, his father standing in the doorway.

Dane's jaw locked. "Dad, could you give us a minute?"

The look on his father's face was grim. That's when Dane noticed that he looked pale and sweaty. Like he'd been running a mile. After recovering from his heart attack, his father had come back to work a few weeks earlier. His father's workload was still light, but maybe it was too much in the wake of his ill health. "We have problem."

Dane frowned. The thought of his father being sick again made his palms start to sweat. "Are you okay?"

"It's not me. I'm fine." His father glanced behind him, and quickly shut the office door. "Nobody can hear us if the door is closed, can they?"

He narrowed his eyes, sensing his father's unease. "Nobody can hear." The argument that was brewing between him and Allyson looked like it would have to wait. "What's going on?"

"I've been looking at the company accounts. Just trying to get back into the swing of things," his father said. "But things don't seem to be adding up."

Allyson's eyebrows furrowed. "What do you mean, Alfred?"

"I think someone has been embezzling funds," his father replied breathlessly. "And from the looks of it, a lot of money has gone missing."

"How much?" Dane asked.

"Tens of millions," his father replied.

Allyson inhaled loudly. "Are you sure?"

His father nodded. "I've checked and rechecked. I'm certain of it. Someone has been skimming money off the top for the past six months. Maybe more, but that's as far back as I've gone."

"Where have they been getting the money from?" she asked.

"That's just it," his father explained, "I can't pinpoint exactly how they're doing it, but I do know they're getting a lot of the money out of the employee pension fund."

Her green eyes grew huge. "*What?*"

"How is that possible?" Dane demanded.

Alfred grimaced. "Whoever it is, I think they're skimming money from employees' pension and benefit accounts, and then funneling it through somewhere. That's why nobody has caught it yet. It probably looks like the money's just getting redistributed rather than taken."

"This is serious." Allyson slumped down into the chair across Dane's desk. "We're going to have to tell the employees. Find out what's going on."

"No," Dane said firmly. "That'll just cause panic. This is inside work. It needs quiet attention, or the guilty parties will run."

"Dane, you can't be serious!" she cried. "We have to tell our employees that their pensions and benefits are disappearing."

"What if Dad's wrong?" he asked. "Look, I trust your judgment, Dad, but I'm the one in charge here. If we're wrong and we make a public announcement like this, the panic could ruin us. Prescott has only just started to get back on sound footing."

"Not to mention bring the police or the feds down us," his father said. "I'm with Dane on this."

"The feds?" she asked. "You mean like the FBI?"

Dane nodded. "A financial crime this big is liable to be huge."

"If it's as bad as I think it is, they could end up hauling us up to D.C." His father ran a hand through his white hair. "This kind of corporate malpractice gets people riled up."

"It should," Allyson said sharply. "People are losing their benefits and pensions. How could something like this have happened?"

"The better question is, how do we stop it?" his father questioned.

Dane scratched his jaw, his thoughts racing a million miles a minute. "What do you mean?"

"As far as I can tell, it's still going on," his father replied. "A million dollars disappeared just last week."

"How are they getting the money out of the company?" Allyson shook her head.

So did Dane. The Handels... now this? Would it ever stop? Or was this the deal with multi-billion-dollar companies... someone was always hunting them down? Would they ever be free of mistrust, embezzlement, stealing, everything? It was exhausting. No wonder his father was so worn out.

"I don't know. I haven't figured that out yet." His father suddenly looked even older. As if the company's problem was aging him right before their eyes.

"Don't tell Mom yet," Dane said. "I'll get someone to look in to this. Someone we can trust."

His father nodded. "I won't."

"We can't keep this information to ourselves forever," Allyson said. "The press might have moved on a bit, but something like this could bring them right back."

Dane frowned.

She was right. After they'd sent the Handels packing back to London, the media had gone into a frenzy for weeks. Then, one of the local basketball teams had been bought by Karl Roth, some new hotshot billionaire, and the New York City press had moved on. A mess like this could bring the scandal-hungry sharks back in a big way.

Allyson was still reeling from her sister-in-law's terrible run-in with the paparazzi. Holly was healthy, and due to give birth in a few weeks, but the press was insatiable and dangerous. As long as a scandal like this was brewing, Dane had to protect his wife and her family at all costs.

"That's why we have to keep this to ourselves for now until I can verify what Dad found," Dane finally said. "I need to make sure, get some more concrete evidence, and figure out who's behind it. I'll look in to it myself, before we get anyone else involved. Keep this between the three of us?"

"The information doesn't leave this room." Allyson nodded in agreement. "Got it. How do we figure out who the thief is, Alfred?"

"I've narrowed it down to the accounts department, some senior executives, and other division and department heads."

"That's, like, forty people," she said.

"And that doesn't exclude any others that those forty people might have purposely or inadvertently tipped off to getting this kind of money." Dane crossed his arms. "How do we start digging for more information?"

His father sighed. "That kind of information is probably somewhere in the accounts department. On a laptop or a memory stick. But there are also hard files with some information that might be useful."

Dane nodded. "Okay. Let's see if we can find a quiet way to get our hands on some information."

"We have to be careful. The only reason I found this out is because I came back to work and was trying to get my bearings. It's not something I would ordinarily have known. Dane, whoever is doing this..."

Terror flickered in his father's brown eyes. "If they discover that we know, we'll be in danger. I think the thief would be willing to do anything to keep this a secret. Even kill."

"DON'T YOU THINK YOUR father was being a little bit paranoid?" Allyson bit her lip, apprehension tying her stomach up in knots. His father had just left the office to go to a business meeting. And hopefully he put on a big show of acting like everything at Prescott Global was still normal.

"The thing is, my dad has a good reason to be scared." Dane was packing away his laptop. "Back in the 1980s, my father lost a friend. His friend was a senior executive who discovered wrongdoing at the corporation he worked at. Right before he went to the press, he was murdered. The wrongdoing came out eventually, but by then it was too late."

She gasped. Her heart started to pound wildly. "That's horrible. Would someone actually try to hurt us like that?"

Her husband looked up from his desk, determination turning his blue eyes glacial. "I'll never let anyone hurt you. Ever." Dane crossed the office and stopped at her seat. He looked down at her, reached for her hands, and pulled her to her feet. When he stared deep into her eyes, she shivered. Shivered under the cold intensity of his eyes. "I would kill to protect you, Allyson."

"I'm sure there's no need for that," she said sharply. Now her entire body was covered in goose bumps. Fear, cold and oily, slipped across her skin. But it wasn't the fear of a desperate thief that was making her react like this. It was the fear of what her husband might do. When Dane got it into his head that he had to protect her, he acted recklessly. Did just about anything to neutralize whatever he thought was a threat to her.

"Look, the problems we've dealt with before are nothing compared to this," he said in a warning tone. "The Handels were underhanded, but nothing they did was illegal. This is dangerous. You have to promise to let me deal with this on my own."

"Your father thinks the thief is desperate enough to kill, and you want me to let you face this alone?" She dragged her hands out of his grasp.

"That's not a request, Allyson," Dane said forcefully. "That's an order."

Anger flared within her. So hot and violent that it chased away the cold fear. "How dare you."

"Allyson—"

"Don't you dare!" she cried. "Don't you dare order me to do anything ever again."

"Fine." His expression hardened. "Don't listen. But I don't have to share the intimate details of what I'm doing with you."

"More secrets," she snapped. "If you want to keep more things from me, you go right ahead. But it's not going to help you. You can build whatever wall you want. I'm not going to give up on you."

"I'm not keeping anything from you," he ground out.

"Really?" She crossed her arms and glared at him. "Why don't you like the house, Dane?"

"Fine. You want to help? Bring the car out back."

"What?"

"I'm going to be taking some documents home," he said through gritted teeth. "I need you to drive the car out of the underground parking lot and head to the lot at the back."

"Why?"

He sighed heavily. "There's a huge blind spot out there that the security cameras don't pick up. Right now, we can't trust anyone. Not even the company security team."

"What are you talking about?" she demanded. "What documents, Dane? What're you up to?"

"I want to smuggle some confidential documents out of here," he said in a low voice, "so that I can confirm my father's suspicions. He's gone over the information digitally, so now I need to go over the physical paper trail. I'd go over the files here at headquarters, but I don't want to risk anyone seeing. Tipping off the thief could make them violent, or make them smart enough to disappear and avoid getting caught. So the best thing to do is take the files home."

"How're you going to smuggle them out without being seen?" she asked. "There are cameras everywhere."

"Not if I take the stairs," he muttered.

"Are you crazy? You can't walk down fifty flights of stairs."

"Sure I can," he replied. "I'm in the best shape of my life. And I owe it all to you."

She rolled her eyes. "Why? Is being married to me that physically taxing for you?"

"Oh, yes. The nightly workouts have been very intense." There was a mischievous glint in his eye.

Her cheeks burned. "I cannot believe you're joking about sex at a time like this."

"It's this, or we go back to arguing and you being defiant for no good reason," he said.

She stifled an exasperated sigh. "Just give me the car keys."

Minutes later, she walked across Prescott Global's underground parking lot, gripping the car keys in her hand. Allyson glanced over her shoulder as discreetly as she could. There were cameras around and she didn't want to give anything away.

Finally, she got to their luxury car, jumped behind the wheel, and turned the ignition. She navigated the car out of the underground parking lot, then drove around to the above-ground parking lot at the back of Prescott. Finally, she parked in the spot Dane had instructed her to park in.

Now, all she had to do was wait. Her heart hammered so wildly against her ribcage she could swear she could hear it. With her hands still gripping the steering wheel, she forced herself to inhale. It was obvious that Dane had asked her to bring the car out back to get her out of the way. The only reason she had agreed to it was because she was still determined to help her husband. Even if he was trying to get her out of the way.

The wait in the car was agonizing. Each moment that ticked by felt like an age. What if someone discovered Dane smuggling the confidential files out of headquarters? There were consequences for removing confidential documents. His contract could be shredded, or he could end up with a lawsuit on his hands.

Worse, this had all started before she got the truth out of Dane. She needed to know why her husband was willing to buy a house he didn't seem to want. Needed to know what secrets he was keeping from her. A crazy thought occurred to her. No. Of course not. There was no way Dane could have known about the embezzlement before his father had revealed it to them. There was no way he'd keep something like that from her.

When the waiting got bad enough for her to consider racing back into the building, her husband finally appeared, a cardboard box in his hands. He got into the passenger seat beside her, breathing heavily.

"Do I drive straight home?" she asked.

He nodded. "Yeah. But don't drive too quickly. Make it look normal. Like we're heading home for lunch."

She pulled out of the parking lot and away from Prescott Global headquarters.

By the time they got home to their apartment, Allyson was a nervous wreck. She couldn't shake the eerie feeling that they were being watched. It was probably paranoia brought on by stress, but she couldn't shake the uneasy feeling.

In the living room, Dane started to take the files out of the box.

She flopped down onto the sofa and whipped out her cell phone to email some of the women's division senior managers. It was all routine work stuff, but right now she needed a distraction while her husband pored over files.

Finally, Dane looked up from his work, his eyebrows furrowed. "We have a massive problem."

"What?" She sat up straighter.

"I figured out how the money is being stolen from Prescott," he said. "It's being funneled out through the women's division."

Chapter 4

The phone she was holding was suddenly heavy in her hands. Allyson's heart sank like a stone.

"Someone in my division is embezzling money?" she finally gasped out.

"I don't know," Dane replied. "Possibly... Probably."

"How could anyone do this?" Bile rose in her throat. The thought of a subordinate stealing from Prescott made her sick to her stomach. Anyone stealing from the company was horrible. Her division, the revamped women's line, had already shown success in the markets. The people working with her seemed like good, solid thinkers. The worst thing anyone from the women's division had done was gossip. But this, millions of dollars stolen, was on a level she couldn't comprehend. Someone they knew and trusted was stealing out of employee funds. She swallowed. "What do we do now? Do we inform the staff that their pensions and benefits are disappearing? It's a lot of money, Dane. It's not something that can stay hidden for long."

He ran his hand through his hair, frustration etched on his face. "If we go public with this, it will cause a company-wide panic. Stocks would crash again. Prescott has only just gotten back on track after that mess with the Handels."

"Our employees have the right to know their benefits are in jeopardy," she repeated. "I'd want to know." She'd paid into the fund before Dane and she had gotten married. Shoot, she still could be paying into the fund. Not that it mattered. But it did matter. So did the company's liability. What were they going to do?

"If stocks crash again, it'll be more than pensions and benefits being in jeopardy," he said. "I don't think we can weather another storm like this. Not six months after the last one. If Prescott gets into trouble now, I can see massive layoffs. And that's without the police and the FBI getting involved."

"So, what do we do?" she asked. "If we don't stop whoever is doing this, they'll keep stealing."

"We have to find the culprit before the media gets wind of this," he said. "If we find out who it is, we can control the narrative. We can hand over the evidence to the police, then keep the press from going into a frenzy. Let's try to handle this as smoothly as possible."

Her nerves were frayed. Worry gnawed at her. "I knew something like this was going to happen."

Dane paused. Focusing his gaze on her he narrowed his eyes. "How could you have known?" he asked, barely able to mask the suspicion in his voice.

"You don't actually think I had something to do with this, do you?" It was impossible to keep the accusation out of her tone. Especially since the guilt weighing down on her was only getting heavier. Earlier, while she had waited for Dane in the car, she had momentarily wondered if he had known about the embezzlement. Wondered if what he was hiding had to do with the theft his father had just uncovered. Now, it sounded like Dane had suspicions of his own.

"I'm not accusing you of anything," he said firmly. "I'm just starting to realize how something like this might look."

"How does it look?" she asked shrilly.

His jaw clenched. Like he was fighting to keep the words in. "It looks bad."

"Oh, really? Does it? How do you particularly see this situation?"

"Come on, Allyson," he said, looking as frustrated as she felt. "The embezzlement started about six months ago. Around the same time you stepped in and revamped the women's division. And now I've just figured out that the money is being funneled through this very same division. Not to mention, you're the division head. Which means you're one of the forty people who has access to the company accounts."

A lump formed in her throat. "You really think I'm capable of something like this?"

"Hell no," he said. "But a lot of people might think you are. A lot of people want to see you stumble. They've been rooting for you to fail ever since we got married."

She slumped back in her seat, completely miserable. The first six months of their marriage had been wonderful. They had worked side by side at Prescott Global. Taken romantic excursions to Niagara Falls and the Grand Canyon. And even though things weren't perfect with her side of the family, Dane had been bonding with her brother James. Meanwhile, she had been working on her relationship with Dane's parents. The few things that seemed to be an issue had been her friends, the new house, and now this new awful mess at Prescott.

"What people?" she breathed. "I've made friends. I've been networking with all these business people. Doors have been opening for me. Who would want to see me fail?"

"Your friends," he replied.

"That's not true."

"I know the upper class better than you do," he said. "They're all throwing themselves at you now, while they secretly resent your success. If news about this embezzlement gets out before we figure out who the actual thief is, don't be surprised if your so-called friends blame you."

"I don't believe that they'd do something like that," she said.

"If it's not your friends, then the rest of the upper class will be happy to see this scandal take you down," he said. "Resentment over new people coming into high society runs deep."

She paused. While it was true that Dane understood the upper class far better than she did, she had been learning. Especially from his mother. "If the upper class is as bad as you say it is, then we need allies.

Right now it's us against a thief we can't see. And it's not even us; it's just you."

"I'm not dragging you into this," he said firmly.

"Last time you didn't want me getting involved in our problems, I eventually ended up helping you," she reminded him.

"That was different. Everything the Handels did was legal. They were underhanded, but they played by certain rules. Whoever is doing this has no qualms about stealing millions. Which means they're either extremely powerful or extremely desperate. Besides, you should focus on moving into the new house."

Unable to hide her irritation, she took a deep breath. "Let me see if I have this right...this embezzlement could literally ruin me, but instead of helping you fix the problem you want me to act like a good little wife and spend my time buying furniture for the new house that you clearly don't like."

He held up his hands. "That's not what I meant."

"You don't think I can handle this."

"I don't want my wife to get hurt," he murmured. "Is that so wrong?"

Except something was wrong. A lot of things seemed suddenly wrong. "Why don't you like the house, Dane?"

His eyebrows rose. Her husband shrugged. "Am I required to like the house?"

"Yes," she said sharply. "You're required to like the house that you're going to be living in. Otherwise, what's the point?"

"It's not the house that's the problem." He sighed.

That made her heart start racing again. Sweat formed on her brow. If the problem wasn't the house, then it was likely that the problem was their marriage. Or worse. Her. Swallowing hard, she asked, "Is it me? Am I the problem?"

"Of course not." Concern flashed in his eyes. "You're not a problem. How could you think that? Have I made you think that?"

"You won't tell me what's wrong," she said softly. "I can feel this wall between us, and I know you're keeping something from me. I can sense it."

He got to his feet, walked over to her, and held out his hand. Anticipation over what he might say made her chest tighten painfully. Reluctantly, she placed her hand in his and let him help her to her feet. She let him lead her out of the living room and over to the balcony. As always, the view of New York City took her breath away. There was a slight chill in the air. The type of chill that was always invigorating. "My contract renewal is coming up," he began. "But working at Prescott just doesn't have the same spark that it once did."

She blinked in surprise. That was the last thing she had been expecting. "You want to quit? Stop working?" Working without her husband made her feel hollow. Like her insides had been carved out and all that was left was an empty shell. Allyson knew it was crazy to feel something so extreme, but part of the joy of working at Prescott was working with the man she loved.

"I don't want to stop working," he said. "It's just that, for the past six months, Prescott hasn't been much of a challenge."

"That's because you've managed everything so well," she pointed out.

"I guess I'm a victim of my own success." He flashed a wry smile.

She bit her lip. "Do you know what you're going to do?"

"I have no idea," he said. "For the first time in my life I have no clue what I want to do with the rest of it."

Sadness made her shoulders slump. He must have noticed how crestfallen she looked, because he wrapped his arm around her and drew her to him. His strong embrace warmed her. Steadied her as she went over his words in her mind.

For six months she had been so happy and fulfilled in her work with the women's division, and the whole time Dane hadn't been nearly as happy about his own work. How had she missed it? How had she not seen her husband's unease until yesterday, during the tour of the house?

"I'm so sorry," she breathed. "You were miserable this whole time and I didn't even notice."

He chuckled. "I wasn't miserable. Not with you. I've been having a hell of a time with you." He planted a warm kiss on her forehead. The tender gesture shot to her heart. "It's just that moving into this new house because it's near Prescott means that—"

"It means you'll be making a big decision based on a job you don't love the way you used to," she finished for him.

"That's right." He nodded.

"Why didn't you tell me?" she asked. "Shouldn't we be able to tell each other everything?"

"Of course," he said. "But you were so proud and happy to be working at Prescott. And I'm proud of you. I knew you would do well after getting the promotion."

"You shouldn't be so concerned about my happiness that you keep things to yourself," she said.

"I probably should have told you," he conceded. "But what's done is done. Now you know."

"Have you decided what you're going to do?"

"If I'm going to catch this thief and deal with the fallout, I'll probably have to renew my contract," he said.

"That means you'll be at Prescott for at least another six months." She lowered her eyes. The guilt was back again. "Six months of more unhappiness. Dane, don't renew the contract."

"I have to protect you," he said. "That's my priority. Always will be."

She pulled away from him and turned to look back through the floor-to-ceiling window of their apartment. Everything inside was so luxurious. So masculine. Like him. This was his world. And now, she was dragging him out of it. Making him live in a house he didn't really want. "If you're going to hunt down the thief, there's no way I can expect you move into the house now. Not if you have to renew a contract you don't want to renew. You'll be trapped because of me."

"Allyson, if I renew my contract, moving into this new house will actually be convenient," he said. "Anyway, I've been looking forward to moving into a new place with you. Besides, I've paid for the house. It's ours now."

"We can always sell it—"

"Not another word," he interrupted. "This is the house of your dreams. I want us to really start our lives together. We're moving in. It's going to be my dream, too."

"You're sure?"

"I'm more than sure."

Her brows pressed together again. "What are we going to do about the embezzlement?"

He raised an eyebrow. "We?"

"You're staying at a job you don't love to help me," she said. "So, yes, this is something we both have to do. I'm not backing down from this."

"I'm not agreeing to anything," he said. "But it sounds like you have one of your famous plans."

She nodded. "I do. The best way to handle this is to call the police. Now."

THE NEXT MORNING, INSTEAD of heading to work like he usually did, Dane escorted his wife into the police station. His father and the Prescott Family lawyer were trailing behind.

Ordinarily, he would never have allowed Allyson to talk him into something like this, but the longer they took to catch the thief the more money they were liable to lose. They'd considered contacting the board last night, and then decided that speaking to the police would be the best step. The less people knew until they had something solid, the better.

A police officer led them to a detective's office and motioned for them to sit on the bench outside. "Detective Rossi will be with you in a minute, so you folks can have a seat." With that, the officer walked off.

After about fifteen minutes Detective Paul Rossi appeared, introduced himself, and ushered them in to a dingy lecture room. There was a podium up front, a white board taking up an entire side wall, and chairs lined up across the room.

Dane had never met the detective, but the family lawyer knew him well enough and had recommended they see him. The only reason Dane was even bothering to trust a police officer was because their lawyer had vouched for him.

Dane took a seat beside his wife while Rossi sat down facing them, a notebook and pencil in hand. The detective was middle-aged, stocky, his dark hair graying at the temples. Rossi regarded them sternly, an air of skepticism radiating off him. "So, folks, what's the trouble?"

Their lawyer cleared his throat and nodded to Dane. Quickly, he rattled off the facts he had managed to gather about the embezzlement, while his father helped fill in some other information.

"And you have the files to prove that the money has gone missing?" Rossi asked.

He nodded. "I've got confidential files in my father's car. I'm not exactly authorized to take them out of Prescott, but I'm willing to risk it and hand them over if needed."

"I can look at them," Rossi said. "But we're going to need a lot more evidence if we're going to catch this guy."

"How do we go about doing that?" Allyson asked.

"We need to narrow it down," Rossi said. "We need to focus on everyone with access and everyone with a motive. Motive plus access is the most important criterion."

"So, someone desperate for money, who has access to the accounts," she said.

"Right. Do you know of anyone who's been having financial diffi-culty?" Rossi asked. "That's the first route. But it might not be some-one desperate for money. Could be someone with a vendetta against you. Or someone who's been doing this for year and only getting caught now. There're a million scenarios. We just need to narrow them down. Let's start with the financial issue first."

"I can't imagine the senior executives or the department heads hav-ing financial trouble," Dane said.

Rossi shrugged. "You never know with people. They live beyond their means. Get into debt."

"That still leaves a lot of suspects," Allyson said with a frown. "We thought of about forty people who could have pulled off something like this."

"Well, then, we need to start eliminating suspects," Rossi said. "We might have to tap some phones."

Allyson's eyes widened. "What?"

"Look, we need to draw people out," Rossi said. "Get a feel for what they're saying and thinking. The thief is never going to open up to any of you, so the best chance we have is to tap the phones."

"Is that the only way?" Dane asked.

"You said you wanted to keep things discreet," Rossi murmured.

Dane nodded. "We do. Prescott has had one too many bad head-lines this year, and we've only just gotten back on sound footing."

"That's why this is the best way," Rossi said. "We'll have to get the feds involved, but tapping the phones keeps things discreet. We can come in. Look like repair guys. Tap the phones. And nobody at Prescott will know. If we go in all guns blazing, we'll scare whoever is doing this into hiding or getting rid of the evidence. This way we figure out who the thief or thieves are."

"It hadn't occurred to me that it could be more than one person," his wife said softly.

Rossi gave her a hard look. "It's probably fewer than three people. More than that and you'd have people revealing the secret. Whoever is doing this is smart. Smart enough to keep this hidden for six months. When did you start this women's division again, Mrs. Prescott?"

"What the hell are you implying?" Dane demanded.

"Whoa." Rossi leaned back. "I'm just doing my job, Mr. Prescott. It sounds to me like a lot of money is flowing through a division that's been getting an awful lot of funding lately. And your wife is in charge of this division. I have to ask questions."

Dane rose to his feet, staring the detective down. He balled up his fists. Felt a volcanic anger rising in him. Getting in a cop's face probably wasn't a good idea, but he wasn't going to let anyone get away with insulting Allyson. He had anticipated that people would suspect her, but it still rankled. Nobody was going to get away with disrespecting his wife. "Do whatever you have to do, but leave my wife out of this."

"We have to do a thorough investigation," Rossi shot back. "You don't have to like it, but there's going to be a list of suspects. And, based on everything I've heard here today, you *and* Mrs. Prescott are my prime suspects."

Chapter 5

He grabbed Allyson's hand and started heading across the lecture room. "I've heard enough."

"Wait." She raced ahead of him to place her hands on his chest. "I know this is hard, but we shouldn't leave."

"I'm not going to stay here and take this," he growled.

Behind him, their lawyer was speaking to Detective Rossi in desperate tones.

"Mr. Prescott, I'll be needing those files," Rossi finally said.

Dane turned around to scowl at the detective. "Why should I keep helping you?"

"Because I did you a favor by giving you a heads up about the wiretapping, despite the fact that you're now one of my top suspects," Rossi replied. "I've scratched your back, now you scratch mine."

He took Allyson's hand again and stalked out of the lecture room with her. There was an exasperated expression on her face, but she said nothing. Probably because she knew that he was on the verge of losing his temper. Not with her, but with Rossi. After making the difficult and dangerous decision to go to the police, this was how they were being repaid. With threats and innuendos.

His blood was still boiling when he and Allyson stepped out of the police station, Dane's father and the family lawyer right on their heels. The black SUV his father often used pulled up to them, the tinted windows coming down.

One of the back doors opened and his father's new assistant, Francesca Barnes, stepped out. He frowned. There was no love lost between Allyson and Fran. Not after she had make disparaging comments about his wife to Katherine Handel, of all people. His father's assistant had interned at Prescott several months earlier and then gotten promoted to assistant when his father returned to work. Allyson had been gracious enough to put aside her misgivings about Fran, but right now he was fuming.

"We need the box," Dane said bluntly to Fran.

Fran nodded and quickly grabbed the cardboard box full of files from the backseat. "I can bring it in for you if you'd like, sir."

He nodded. "That'll be fine, thank you. You can go inside with the lawyer."

With Fran and their lawyer disappearing back into the station, Dane helped Allyson into the car and got into the back seat beside her. His father sat up front.

"That could have gone better," his father muttered.

"What's done is done," Allyson said softly.

Suddenly, a shifty-looking man in a grey trench coat appeared, sticking his hand in through the window by Allyson. "Mrs. Prescott! I'm a photojournalist with the *New York City Inquirer* and I was wondering if you'd like to comment—"

"You've been following us?" Dane's eyes narrowed.

"I'm not at liberty to say," the photojournalist responded. Then, he actually grabbed Allyson's arm. "What do you say? How about a quote?"

Before Allyson could pull her arm away Dane lunged across the backseat, shoved the door open, and grabbed the photojournalist by the collar. He swore loudly. "Touch my wife again and I'll destroy you."

The photojournalist struggled in his grasp. "And I'll sue." He swallowed. "Fine. You've made your point. Let me go."

"Dane, don't hurt him," Allyson pleaded. "Don't cause a scene. Not here. Not now."

"You're lucky my wife is such a sweet and gentle person," Dane snarled before shoving the photojournalist away. He didn't bother to watch to see what the creep did. He got back into the car, fury rippling through him. By the time his father's assistant and their lawyer returned, Dane was so angry he could barely think straight. Nobody said anything. The tension in the car was palpable.

The SUV pulled down the street.

"That wasn't wise," his father said, finally breaking the silence. "The media's just going to start digging in earnest now. We probably only have days before the story breaks. I have no choice but to call Detective Rossi and warn him about the press."

"Sometimes, I really can't stand this town," Dane muttered.

Without a word, Allyson reached over and placed her hand on top of his. Her touch was soothing. Calming. Made the anger that had been roiling through him start to recede.

"What do we do?" she asked. "About the media? If the story breaks soon, it could be really bad for Prescott."

"We can make some preliminary statements to the press," Dane said. "Try to control things before rumors spread."

"That's fine, but you two should probably lay low for the next few days," his father said. "Better to keep your heads down in case some unsavory speculation about your involvement with this comes out."

"Lay low?" Dane asked.

"Don't stay in your apartment," his father instructed. "That's the first place the press will go."

"Where on earth can we go?" Allyson asked, her voice trembling.

Dane gritted his teeth. "I have an idea where we can stay."

SHE STARED INTO THE fire. Stuck her hands out to let the flames warm her. "It works!"

Dane grinned. "See?" His voice echoed across the mostly empty living room.

After the awful time at the police station, they had spent the day at work. They had only just settled in for the night in the new house. There wasn't much by way of furniture yet but her new assistant, Cameron, had helped her bring some essential items here so they could do their best and lay low in case news of the embezzlement broke. Cameron was a Godsend. He'd gotten them supplies, toiletries, a food stash, and extra clothes, not to mention the sleeping bags.

"I've never lived in a house with a fireplace before," she said.

He stopped stoking the fire to sit down beside her on the sleeping bag. "Now you have one of your own."

But for how long? Talking to that detective earlier today had unnerved her. She knew that she might end up a suspect. Especially after Dane had warned her about how suspicious she would look. It made sense, and the police wouldn't be doing their job if they didn't take a good hard look at everyone on staff. Still, she hated that Detective Rossi had not only suspected her, but Dane as well.

If something went wrong, and the police blamed them for the embezzlement, they could end up in a world of trouble.

"I'm sorry about what happened at the police station," she said softly.

He gave her an incredulous look. "What do you have to be sorry for?"

"It was my idea to tell the police, and Detective Rossi suspected you," she said. "I wanted to help you so badly, but I just got you into a bigger mess."

"It's done now." Wrapping his arm around her shoulders, he pulled her close. "I don't like you getting mixed up in all this, but going to the police was probably our best option. At least we look like we're trying to be transparent and the cops can't accuse us of a cover-up."

A sigh escaped her lips. "I just worry that we might get in trouble. Like, no matter what happens, they'll end up blaming us. Say we're liable, because we were negligent and didn't see the embezzlement sooner."

"We've done our best to prevent any kind of scandal," Dane said. "That's why going to the police was the right call. Plus, we have a good team of lawyers."

The photojournalist who had harassed them outside the police station would probably chase down the story. After Dane had gotten in the guy's face, he was probably out for revenge. Breaking the story about an embezzlement case would be a juicy enough scandal to satisfy that. Especially if the media found a way to spin things and blame her or Dane for the crime.

"What happens when the story breaks?" she asked.

"Dad warned the detective that the press might find out, so right now everything is up to the police," he replied. "They'll be tapping the company phones within the next few days. All we can do now is wait to see what they discover."

"Are you still going to sign your contract renewal?" She leaned against him, loving how safe his solid presence made her feel.

"Yes," he said. "Right now, it's my job to protect the staff. We can't risk telling anyone else at Prescott about the embezzlement yet, because then the thief might hide or get rid of the evidence. So, the staff has no idea that things with the company are going to be rocky. It wouldn't be fair for me to abandon them right before the police start an investigation like this."

"I wish there was a way to avoid the worst of it," she said.

"The best thing we can do is let the police handle things," he said.

"Even though they suspect us?" she asked.

He frowned. "I don't like how that cop talked to you today. But after they tap the phones, they'll have to figure out the truth."

"Just don't antagonize the police," she begged. "I don't want them going after you—"

"I'm not going to put up with anyone disrespecting you," he cut in sharply. "As long as the cops do their job, they have nothing to worry about."

What worried her was what her husband might do if the police didn't do their job. She had wanted to involve the police so that everything was transparent and above board. Only, that had backfired because the police now suspected them of embezzling. Allyson had wanted to do the right thing, and now it felt like they were both being punished for it.

"I'm just worried," she confessed. "These last few months with you have been so wonderful, but now we have to deal with this mess."

He pulled back to cup her face in his hands. "As long as we have each other, everything is worth it."

She smiled. Dane traced his thumb across her lips and she trembled in response. No matter how afraid she got, knowing that she had her husband's strength inspired a courage inside her that she'd never had before she met him. Allyson was already melting under his touch, and her eyes fluttered closed. When she felt his lips press against hers, a low moan sounded in her throat.

Allyson wanted him now. Desperately. Completely. The wall he had built up between them had been slowly crumbling since he confessed to not loving his job any more. There was a twinge in her heart at the thought of him being unhappy. But his delicious kiss chased those thoughts away.

As she opened her eyes she wrapped her arms around him, fusing her body to his. The place between her thighs throbbed with indescribable need. Already she was wet, her arousal taking over every inch of her body.

He dragged his mouth away to start kissing her neck. Each kiss warmed her and made her shiver at the same time. Slowly she started to lie back on the sleeping bag, pulling him down on top of her.

Dane stopped his kissing to stare deep into her eyes. "You're not going to be too cold, are you?"

She laughed and shook her head. "Not with you here to warm me up."

With a wolfish grin, her husband pulled at her sweater and helped her get it off. Then, he peeled away her jeans. She was down to nothing but her underwear. Somehow, right before her eyes, his clothes melted away until he was naked before her. His blond hair fell over his hungry eyes, every inch of his perfectly sculpted body making her mouth water.

When he lay on his side beside her she glanced down at his erection, a blush rising in her cheeks. No matter how many times they did this, Dane still had the ability to make her blush like a schoolgirl.

Quickly, she sat up to reach behind her to unhook her bra and then peel off her panties. When she lay back down, her head lay on his outstretched arm. She reached for his other arm and slowly started to guide his hand down to her throbbing sex. Wantonly, she spread her legs.

Dane's eyebrow quirked up and he flashed a lazy smile. "Is that what you want?"

A giggle escaped her throat and she nodded. "Yes."

He eased a finger into her slick, wet heat. Intense pleasure made her arch her back involuntarily. One touch already had her losing control. As he swirled his finger into her, she clenched around him. Her lips parted, but the sound of her ragged moan was lost as he teased her mouth open with his tongue.

The ecstasy he was giving her with his hand had her body quivering. The way his tongue swirled in her mouth as he eased another finger into her already had her on the edge. But it wasn't enough. She ached to have more of him. To be under him.

She pulled her lips away to gasp, "Dane. I want you." She whimpered, "Now. *Please.*"

Dane slipped his hand away from her and positioned himself between her legs. Wrapping her thighs around his waist, she guided him into her. She was crushed beneath his hard, solid body, and the delicious weight of her husband on top of her was already driving her wild.

He groaned as he thrust into her slowly, each powerful stroke filling her with more pleasure than the last. Desperately, she wrapped her arms around him, holding on to him tightly as he started to rock into her harder. Faster. Bliss consumed her. Unraveled her until she was trembling. Moaning his name. Having him like this on top of her showed her just how much he was willing to give. He always gave his all to her. Didn't hold back as his body gave her pleasure.

The sensation of his hot skin on hers pushed her over the edge, her climax coming hard and fast. When he stared deep into her eyes he forced out a ragged breath, climaxing right after her.

Spent, he slipped off her and pulled her onto his chest. He was breathing so hard that when she placed her cheek on his torso, she felt his chest heave with each intake of breath. Her own heart was racing so fast she felt like it might explode.

Finally, his labored breathing slowed, and he gently kissed her forehead. That made her smile.

"I guess we christened the house," Dane said.

She laughed, the sound bouncing off the walls. "I guess we did."

They had just made love for the first time in their new home, and knowing that touched her still-racing heart. This house already meant so much to her, but now she knew their love was what was going to make it a real home. A home and a refuge from the craziness of living an upper-class life. Someday they would add even more love to the house, and settle down to have their children. In her husband's arms she felt so content that she hardly knew what to do with herself.

"I love you," she breathed.

"And I love you," he said.

"Are you ready for the awards ceremony?" she asked, reminding him of the prize he was going to be given over the weekend.

"Honestly, with all this stuff going on at work this week, I forgot," he said.

She snuggled up to him. "I haven't forgotten. I'm so proud of you, Dane." Despite his heart not being completely into Prescott Global, over the past six months he had done so much for the company. Saved countless jobs. Kept Prescott from going into debt. Made sure the investors were happy. The fact that he hadn't been thrilled about it reminded her of what a caring, selfless man her husband was. Now he was going to renew his contract, just so he could make sure the company's employees were well taken care of.

"Thanks," he said.

"You deserve it," she said.

He grinned. "I think you're more excited about this than I am."

"It's because I have a speech ready," she said.

He groaned. "I forgot about the speech. What are you going to say about me?"

"I'm going to gush over you, of course," she said with a smile.

"You're obviously biased." He chuckled.

"Of course, I am," she said. "I have a thing for strong, capable men. Naturally, I'd take a liking to you."

"I knew you had a crush on the boss," he teased.

"Can you blame me?" She rained kisses down on his face, enjoying the feel of his stubbled jaw against her skin.

His laughter was cut short by his cell phone ringing. Dane groaned again. Reluctantly he reached for his pants to yank his phone out of the pocket.

He sat up to answer it. "Dane Prescott." His blue eyes narrowed. "Oh. It's you. What do you want?"

Sitting up straighter she hugged her knees, wondering who could be making her husband this agitated already. Her heart froze at the thought that it might be bad news from work. Or worse, the police.

"No, I'm not giving you anything," he muttered. "And neither is my wife."

Chapter 6

H e hung up the phone and shot to his feet.

"Who was that?" Allyson asked.

Dane reached for his clothes and started to get dressed. "A newspaper editor." The fact that the editor himself had been brazen enough to call meant that whatever they had on Prescott was concrete. Damn it. He knew the media would get wind of the embezzlement story soon, but this was even sooner than he'd anticipated.

She sighed. "These tabloids are relentless."

"It wasn't a tabloid," he said shaking his head. "It was one of the respectable newspapers. They've been digging around for a story. They're looking for someone to corroborate the rumors about the embezzlement."

"How do they know already?"

"My guess is that detective talked to the press," he muttered. Anger flared. Going to the police had probably been the right call, but it had been a mistake to trust that they'd keep the story to themselves.

"You really think a police officer would do that?" she asked. "Wouldn't something like that put his job in jeopardy?"

"It's possible that the detective told a tabloid in exchange for money," he said. "We have no way of knowing for sure, but I'm guessing that's how the more legitimate newspapers got wind of it."

"So...what did the editor want?"

"He promised to spin the embezzlement story in our favor if we gave him something better," he said. "They're looking for an even bigger story."

"What on earth could be bigger?" she asked.

"They seem to think we know who the thief is," Dane said. "If we give the details on who the thief is, they won't blame us for mishandling the crime."

She groaned. "This is bad."

"It gets worse," he said grimly. "They think we have something to do with the embezzlement. That's the story they want to run with. Basically, an exposé blaming you and me for the problem, and accusing us of keeping it from the company for months."

"But we've only just found out. We have nothing to do with the embezzlement. We had no idea." She started to pull her clothes back on.

The truth wasn't going to stop the media from printing all kind of innuendos. Detective Rossi had said it himself: he and Allyson were the prime suspects. It wouldn't matter if Allyson had been a media darling these past few months. Nobody would care that they had tried to do the right thing by reporting the matter to the police. Scandal was what sold newspapers and drove headlines.

"They won't care about the real story," he said. "Right now, we have to inform the board. Even if one of them might be the thief, we have to let them in on what we know before the story blows wide open in the media. Then we can leak some information to the press. Get the word out that the police are involved and we're addressing the problem head-on."

She stood up and nodded. "Right. Show that we don't have anything to hide. You did the right thing not taking the newspaper editor's bait."

"The problem with this mess is that even when something is the right thing, it feels wrong," he said forcefully. "It's like every choice is a bad choice."

"Well, with the awards ceremony coming up this week, we can use it as an opportunity to get some good press," she said. "Show that Prescott is united and moving forward." She bit her lip. "I'll have to amend my speech. Make reference to the fact that people might have heard rumors, but we're working on protecting the company."

"What about the staff?" he asked. "If news about the embezzlement really does get out, their jobs could be in jeopardy. Dealing with someone raiding their pensions and benefits is bad enough, but if the investors are spooked they might insist on layoffs."

"I wish there was a way to help..." Allyson wrapped her arms around him tightly.

Holding her close always reminded him that, no matter how bad things got, she was right beside him. Her fierce, stubborn support sometimes infuriated him, but he was nothing without it. Nothing without her. She was the one who inspired him to keep going. To keep trying to help the staff, as if they were all a family. Even if his heart wasn't in the company like it had once been, the employees would always be important to him. "I'm going to set aside some of my own money to make up for the loss."

She stood on her tiptoes to brush her lips against his. With a smile she said, "I don't know how Prescott could ever survive without you." She paused. "If you do want to step down after all this is over, the company will be fine. I just meant..."

He kissed her again. "I know, honey. I know."

ALLYSON WOULD NEVER get used to these fancy events. She glanced around at the crowd that was seated in the auditorium. New York's business elite seemed to have all turned up for Dane's award, despite the rumors floating around.

A crowd full of so many privileged people always frayed her nerves. Even with all the private etiquette lessons she had been taking over the past six months, her insides were in knots. She reached for the glass of water on the table and took a sip of the cold liquid. Hopefully, the water would have get her nerves under control. Tonight was supposed to be Dane's night. Allyson didn't want to ruin it with her jitters.

"You look so beautiful," her husband whispered into her ear.

His warm breath against her skin sent a delighted tingle through her. The strapless dress she had on was elegant and understated. Because tonight was about her husband, she had settled on a basic black evening gown and a pair of black gloves, complete with pearl jewelry. A year ago, she never could have imagined that she would be able to afford an outfit like this. Not to mention, this event was so exclusive she knew the only way she had access to it was because she was Dane's wife.

Pushing aside the doubts about her unearned privilege and lack of achievements, she reached for her husband's huge hand and squeezed it encouragingly. Dane looked positively gorgeous sitting beside her dressed in a tux, his wavy golden hair slicked back.

"And you look perfect," she whispered back.

"Ready to give your speech tonight?"

"Yes, I'm ready," she said with more confidence than she felt. Butterflies fluttered around in her stomach. She had written and rewritten her speech. Gone over it in front of a mirror a thousand times. Even got a public speaking coach to help her. That didn't do much to ease her sudden rush of anxiety. Soon, she would have to get up, walk up onto the stage several feet away, and speak in front of all these people.

Worst of all, even though the press hadn't released the story about the embezzlement, Dane had informed Prescott Global's board. The board hadn't kept the secret for long, and New York's business community was already buzzing with rumors. The police had also showed up at Prescott yesterday and discreetly started tapping company phones. Only she, the police, Dane, his father, and their lawyer knew about the tap, so that rumor hadn't gotten out. Yet.

"I know how much you've been practicing," her husband said. "You're always well-prepared. I know you're going to give a terrific speech."

She set her glass down, letting his words wash over her. The butterflies weren't fluttering as much. Dane's belief in her was already lifting her spirits. Making her feel better. Like she could do anything. "Thanks," she said with a tiny smile.

The other guests at their table were busy chatting excitedly. Dane's parents were sitting on the other end, having a conversation with his father's assistant, Francesca Barnes, and her parents. Ordinarily, assistants got into events like this if they were on the clock and working for their bosses, but Fran was from an illustrious family. It was well known that the Barnes family had lost most of its fortune, but they still had a lot of clout. They still moved in upper-class circles. That was how rich they had been. Despite the humiliation of the loss, the upper class still invited them to events like this.

Allyson swallowed a frown at the sight of Francesca grinning from ear to ear. Fran wasn't exactly a nice person, and had been an ally of that awful Katherine Handel. Still, tonight was about Dane; she wasn't going to let Francesca Barnes dampen her spirits.

Besides, some of her friends were also seated at the table. Gordon and Martha Faraway were her closest friends in high society, and they had showed up to support Dane despite his obvious dislike of them.

Martha, who was sitting next to her, smiled and glanced at the pearl bracelet she wore around her gloved wrist. "That's a lovely bracelet, Allyson," Martha murmured.

She returned her friend's smile and said, "Thank you. I've been looking for an excuse to wear it."

"Well, it suits you," Martha said. "You look lovely tonight."

"So do you," Allyson said, motioning to her friend's beautiful burgundy evening gown. "That's a gorgeous color on you."

Martha's smile widened. "You've got the best taste out of any woman I know, Allyson, so I can rest easy now."

Martha was a makeup heiress named after her famous grandmother, who had started a makeup empire during Hollywood's golden age.

As a New York socialite, Martha had been a staple of the gossip rags since she was a teenager. Now in her late thirties, the auburn-haired beauty was glamorous and sophisticated, but also unpretentious and very bubbly. Allyson had taken a liking to her because of her fun-loving nature. That nature had seemed to be thing that Dane most distrusted, but Allyson appreciated having a friend in high society who wasn't such a stickler for outdated rules.

Finally, they were served dinner. Once they ate and the tables were cleared, the speeches started. Allyson inhaled deeply, trying to calm herself for when it was her turn. Her speech was going to be the one that introduced Dane, so she knew she had to nail it. After all he had done to save Prescott Global from ruin, he deserved to have a memorable speech. Especially considering that he was probably going to be staying on at the company for several more months, even though his heart wasn't in it. The sacrifices he was willing to make for the company were proof that he deserved this award. Deserved to be recognized by his peers.

When the emcee called her to the stage, her heart started to race. Dane gave her an encouraging smile, and that gave her a boost of confidence.

As the crowd applauded, she slowly rose to her feet and walked across the auditorium to the stage. The emcee gave her his arm to help her up the stage until, finally, she stood at the podium.

Fighting the trepidation, she gazed out at the crowd. She hadn't known these people for very long, but they had gathered to honor her husband. That knowledge gave her strength and, taking a deep breath, she began her speech.

The audience laughed at the right moments. Clapped at the tender moments. And through it all Dane focused his attention on her, his encouraging smile making her feel stronger and stronger.

When she wound down the speech to begin her husband's introduction, an audible gasp from the crowd broke her concentration. Several men in police uniforms had forced their way into the auditorium.

Her mouth went dry. What on earth was going on?

Before she could speak, the police officers marched across the room and muscled their way onto the stage. Her chest tightened.

"What's happening?" she cried at one of the officers. "Why are you here?"

"Allyson Prescott?" one of the officers asked gruffly.

She nodded. "Yes."

The officer grabbed her arms, and pain shot up her shoulders. "You're under arrest," he began.

"What?" Her eyes widened in horror. She struggled to break free of the officer's grasp, but he was already slapping handcuffs on her.

The officer started to pull her off the stage while the crowd in the auditorium looked on, outraged expressions on their faces.

"Dane!" she shouted.

Already, her husband was marching towards her. But it was no use. As the police surrounded her and dragged her off the stage, she knew there was nothing anyone could do to save her.

Chapter 7

For the first time in her life, Allyson knew what it was like to be a bird in a cage. Her back ached, her neck was stiff, and she felt like the bars of the holding cell were closing in on her. She'd been quietly crying all night, unable to sleep in the crowded jail cell.

Most of the other women in the cell around her kept to themselves. Some of them had a haunted, glassy look in their eyes. Others were stumbling around drunk. One of them puked on the floor. None of them were dressed in designer couture like she was. She felt like she stood out like a sore thumb.

She shifted on the cold bench, trying to sit in a comfortable position despite her aching muscles.

An officer approached the cell door and peered inside. Her heart leapt, hope consuming her.

"Allyson Prescott?" he called out.

She hurried over to him, avoiding eye contact with the other inmates. The last thing she wanted now was to get on someone's bad side. "Yes," she said breathlessly as she gripped the bars.

"You can get your phone call now." The officer unlocked the door and she slipped out.

All her life, she had taken her freedom for granted. She would never make that mistake again. One night in a holding cell had taught her the ultimate lesson. Freedom was the most precious thing she had. And she wasn't sure if freedom would be guaranteed to her ever again.

The officer led her away from the cell to a wall lined with phones. He motioned for her to sit in front of a phone.

Swallowing hard, she asked, "Who should I call? Do I call my lawyer or—"

"Whoever you want," the officer replied with a shrug.

Dane. There was nobody else in the world she wanted to speak to more than she wanted to speak to her husband. Hands trembling, she sat down and started to dial his number. Each ring made her heart plummet at the thought of him not answering. Never answering.

"Hello." The sound of his deep voice nearly made her collapse in a weeping fit, but she forced herself to stay strong.

"Dane," she breathed. "It's me."

"Thank goodness you're okay," he said. "I showed up to the police station, but they wouldn't let me see you. I've been driving around, circling the block for most of the night."

She gripped the handset tightly. "You're...you're outside?"

"Yes."

All night she had cried, terror making her sob like she never had in her life. She had horrible thoughts of never seeing Dane ever again, and the entire time he'd been outside waiting for her. Biting back a sob she said, "Oh Dane, it's awful. I don't know what to do. I don't even know why I'm in here."

"They're charging you with embezzlement. Against the company. We're going to fight this," he said firmly. "I'm going to be sending the lawyer to you and I'm not leaving. I don't care if they won't let me see you, I'm staying put."

"What about work?" she asked.

"What about it?" He sighed. "Allyson, you have to stop worrying about everyone else and focus on you. Forget work. Forget Prescott. All that matters is getting you out of there."

"Okay." She took a deep breath, bracing herself. "So, you're sending a lawyer?"

"Yes," he replied. "This lawyer is different from the family lawyer. It makes sense, so everything doesn't get tangled up."

She knew what he meant. Better for her to have her own lawyer separate from the Prescott family lawyer, so she didn't drag them all down with her. "How am I going to get out of here?"

"The lawyer will deal with the bail," he said. "But there's more."

Cold sweat broke out along her skin. It was like this nightmare was never-ending. Just when things got really bad, it seemed as if there was something worse right around the corner. She looked over her shoulder, and spied the police officer still hovering behind her. He could probably hear everything she was saying, which meant she had to be careful. "What is it?"

"My father did some digging and found something. He thinks the money that's being embezzled is going out of the country."

"What?" she gasped. That was bad. Very bad. "How am I going to clear my name if the problem is out of the country? If I have embezzlement charges hanging over my head, how on earth can I leave the country to get to the bottom of this?"

"You can ask your lawyer to see if the judge will grant you permission to leave the country," Dane said. "The judge might decline, but it's the best plan we have right now."

Her lower lip trembled. Panic gripped her heart. This was insane. Hours ago, she was at a high-society event, about to hand her husband an award, and now they were talking about begging a judge to let her leave the country to save her from prison. "What do I do now?" she asked softly.

She hated being so vulnerable and dependent, but she could feel her strength slipping away. Leaning on Dane right now sounded so wonderful. Without her husband, there was no way she was going to be able to make it through this.

"Sit tight," he murmured. "The lawyer's name is Lester Crane, and he should be down there soon."

"Okay."

"Oh, and Allyson?"

She bit her lip. "Yes?"

"Whatever you do, don't tell the cops anything. Not a word," he said.

"But I'm innocent," she said, unable to hide the desperation in her voice. "I have nothing to hide. I haven't done anything wrong."

"The police don't care," he bit out. "They don't care about the truth. They don't care about you. Not a word, do you understand?"

"Yes," she said with a nod.

"I know it sounds harsh but I need to give you as much information as I can, so you can protect yourself," he said.

"I understand," she said.

"I'm going to go. I'll call the lawyer now," he said, his tone suddenly sad.

"Thank you."

"Allyson... I love you."

Tears pricked the back of her eyes. No matter how hard she tried to keep herself from crying, tears started to roll down her cheeks. Her heart almost stopped, the fear and sadness were so crushing. "I love you, too," she choked out.

Then he hung up. She leaned forward, her forehead pressed against the phone, and she began to sob.

The officer behind her placed an enormous calloued hand on her bare shoulder. "We need to see you for questioning."

She sucked in a breath, hung up the phone, and got to her feet. "I'm not answering any questions without my lawyer present. He should be here shortly."

The police officer narrowed his eyes and then nodded. "You'll have to go back into the holding cell until he shows up."

"That's fine," she said, suppressing a shudder at the thought of being locked up again. It was obvious that he was trying to scare her into doing an interview without her lawyer, but she wasn't going to fall for it.

No matter how terrified she was of being in the holding cell again, she could wait for her lawyer.

With a curt nod, the officer led her back to the cell and slammed the door shut again behind her. She resumed her seat on the bench and waited. It was impossible to tell how much time had passed, but it felt like hours before the police officer returned with a tall, stern-looking man behind him.

The officer let her out of the holding cell and the stern man introduced himself. "Mrs. Prescott? I'm Lester Crane." He held out his hand, and she shook it gratefully.

"Thank you for coming," she said.

"Not a problem," he said. "That's what I'm paid for."

Together, they followed the police officer into an empty interview room. Allyson took a seat at the table in the center of the room and Lester settled in beside her.

She studied him, doing her best to figure out just how competent he was. Lester was bone-thin, had dark, bushy eyebrows, dark eyes, and a face that looked like it was cut from marble. It was hard to tell how old he was, but she guessed that he was in his forties. He had an intimidating presence, and she hoped that would be to her benefit.

"What's the strategy?" she asked.

Lester put a finger to his lips and narrowed his eyes. "The room might be empty, but you never know who might be listening in."

A cold, creeping dread slid down her spine. Suddenly, the unshakeable sense of being watched seized her. "Right."

"I've gone over everything with Mr. Prescott," Lester said. "Do I have your permission to answer all questions and speak on your behalf?"

She nodded. "Yes. Of course."

Soon, the interview room door swung open and Detective Rossi stepped inside.

The sight of him made Allyson's blood run cold. She had been the one to suggest they tell the police about the embezzlement. She had tried to do the right thing. Follow the rules. And that decision had led to such disastrous results. Rossi wasn't interested in stopping the thief or getting the truth. She couldn't figure out what his agenda was, but it was now clear that it wasn't justice. What a fool she had been to trust the system. What a fool she had been to follow the rules.

Detective Rossi greeted them before he sat down on the other side of the table, but Allyson remained stone-faced. She wasn't going to be nice to him, but she wasn't going to give him the satisfaction of seeing her in distress either.

"So, we have a few questions for you, Mrs. Prescott," Rossi said. "First of all, I just want to say I know how hard this must be for you."

She narrowed her eyes, remembering her husband's warning. The police didn't care about her. They didn't care about the truth. She pressed her lips tightly together in response.

"Come on, you can talk to me," Rossi said. "I'm on your side. I want to help you stay out of prison."

"You don't talk directly to my client," Lester warned. "You have any questions, you'll ask through me. Are we clear?"

Rossi held his hands up. "Crystal clear. My first question is, where are you stashing the money?"

Lester glanced at her. "My client refutes all charges."

Rossi frowned. "I know you think your money and your fancy lawyer will save you, Mrs. Prescott, but it's clear that you've had a hand in this."

Anger coursed through her veins, making her blood boil. How dare he insinuate that she was capable of something so horrible. "If I have so much money, what could my motive for embezzling possibly be?" she demanded.

"That's enough," Lester warned her forcefully. "My client has not admitted guilt."

Rossi gave her a dark, dangerous smile that set her on edge. "You don't come from money. Your position in the upper class isn't assured the way it is for your rich husband. Skimming a little money off the top would give you some wealth of your own, independent of your husband."

She wanted to point out that Dane had set aside a trust for her and she had more money than she could spend in a lifetime. The trust meant she had no reason to steal money, since she had plenty of her own. But she suspected giving him information about her finances would just give the detective more ammunition to use against her. Blurting out the question about motive had been a mistake, and she wasn't about to make another one.

The truth was, reminding the world that she had originally been middle-class would only make things harder for her. Her new-found wealth had given her a false sense of security, but it was obvious that she would never shake off her humble beginnings. She hadn't been born rich, and that seemed to be enough to put her under a cloud of suspicion.

Rossi peppered her with more questions that Lester answered curtly, giving the detective very little information. When the interview was finally over, Lester rose to his feet.

"We'll be posting bail now," Lester said.

Rossi nodded, and gestured for them to follow him as he got to his feet. As she walked out of the interview room and headed towards the front desk of the jail, hope started to make her heart race. She was getting out. Putting this wretched place behind her. For now, at least.

Lester started to talk to the officer at the front desk and Rossi stalked off, leaving them.

"How much is the bail?" Allyson asked softly when Lester turned to her.

"One hundred thousand dollars," Lester replied. If the amount stunned him, he didn't show it. Just rattled off the sum like he was reading off a shopping list.

His cell phone went off and he quickly reached into his jacket pocket to retrieve it. He held up his phone to read a message and frowned. "That's not good."

"What is it?"

"Your husband messaged to inform me that reporters have just gathered outside," Lester murmured. "There are news vans up and down the block."

Bile rose in her throat. She was going to be sick. The thought of facing cameras and reporters unnerved her. "Isn't there a way to sneak out of here?"

Lester shook his head. "No. Even if there was, I don't think sneaking out would be a good idea."

"But all the cameras..."

He placed his hands on her shoulders. "When you go out there, you're going to hold your head up high. Don't make any comments. Let me do the talking."

"Okay." She took a deep breath. "Mr. Crane, if I end up in prison, how long will I be in there?"

"The truth is, I'm going to work on getting you a plea deal," he replied. "None of this has to go to trial."

"A plea deal? You mean, like, say I did it?" She frowned. "But I'm innocent. I didn't do this."

"I know that. But if you don't take a deal, you risk going to trial. And if you lose, you could end up in prison for thirty years."

"*What?*" The world seemed to tilt. Her lungs constricted, and she could hardly breathe. "What happens if I take the plea deal?"

"The maximum would probably be three years. Less if you take good behavior into account," Lester replied. "But we'll discuss strategy as soon as we've posted bail and gotten you out of here."

Her body started to go numb. Every sound in the jail was now distorted, like she'd stuck her head in a blender. Thirty years. Three decades. Behind bars. By the time she got out she'd be in her sixties.

Two hours later, they posted bail and Lester led her outside. A sea of reporters descended on them. Flash bulbs went off, nearly blinding her. The crush of reporters around her nearly sent her into a panic. Avoiding the accusing stares of the crowd, she trained her eyes straight ahead.

"Did you do it, Mrs. Prescott?"

"Are you guilty?"

"Is your husband going to leave you now?"

"How much did you steal? How long have you been taking it?"

"What happened in prison?"

"Did your husband make you take the money?"

"You greedy bi—"

"Enough!" her lawyer shouted calmly. "Mrs. Prescott has no comment at this time." He guided her through the throng of people.

The reporters bombarded her with more questions. Questions about whether she was a thief. Whether she and Dane were getting divorced. If she was a gold-digger who had only married him for his money. She forced herself to tune them out as she walked towards the SUV that was waiting for her.

Dane stepped out of the SUV and helped her inside. Even with her husband's big, strong hands guiding her, she barely felt his touch. Barely acknowledged him. As the SUV pulled away from the mad frenzy of reporters, a terror she never knew existed knifed through her. Now, all she wanted to do was scream.

Chapter 8

His wife slept all day.

Dane was in the living room, poring over documents, when she appeared from their bedroom. Seeing her here in their apartment made the relief he felt more stark. For one night he had thought there was a chance he'd never see her again. It was crazy, he knew, but that she'd been arrested... it didn't make sense, and scared the shit out of him.

The memory wouldn't leave him. It flashed before his eyes over and over.

The police had rushed into the awards ceremony and just hauled her off. He'd gone after them. Tried to see her in jail, but they'd barred him from seeing her. That had sent him into a near-murderous rage, which only calmed down when his father begged him to focus on saving his wife.

"You're awake," he said. Cringed. It was so stupid and obvious, but he had no clue what to say to her. Her ordeal had been harrowing. Hustling her into the car and away from the press had been bad enough, so jail must have been unbearable for her.

She nodded and sank into the sofa across from him. "I didn't get a wink of sleep last night." She yawned. "I slept now, but still feel exhausted."

"You must be hungry," he said. "I've ordered take-out for you."

"Thank you. I'll eat later." Her face was wan. Those dazzling green eyes of hers seemed darker somehow. As if the light had gone out of them. "What are you doing?"

"Trying to figure out where exactly this money is going," he muttered. "Sorry. Stupid, I know."

"Trying to clear my name already?" She gave him a shaky smile.

"No." His jaw clenched. "I'm trying to figure out where it's going so that, when I turn myself in, I can prove that I did it."

She stiffened. "What the hell are you talking about?"

"I'm not letting you go to prison," he said. "We'll tell them I did this."

"No. Absolutely not."

He crossed his arms. "This isn't up to you."

"You can't take the fall for me," she said. "This is my problem, and I'll deal with it. You didn't do this. Neither did I."

Last night had been the worst night of his life. But when his father had managed to calm him down, he knew the only solution was to save Allyson from prison. Save her by going in her place. He refused to watch as her life was destroyed. He had dragged her into his world of wealth. There was no way in hell he was going to let her pay for something she hadn't done.

"I'm not asking your permission," he said bluntly. "I've made up my mind."

"You're crazy if you think I'm going to let you do this." She squared her shoulders and glared.

"Nobody lets me do anything," he said, his voice like ice. "This is my decision."

"My lawyer is working on this," she said. "Mr. Crane suggested a plea deal, but I'm not going to take it. I think we can clear my name by figuring out where the money is going, and find out who the real thief is."

"That's your big plan?" he demanded. "Go on a wild goose chase for a thief who's probably in another country? Risk spending decades in prison because of your pride?"

"If you expect me to consider a plea deal, then you don't know me at all."

He stood up. Headed over to the liquor cabinet on the other side of the living room and grabbed a bottle of scotch. "Maybe I don't. Maybe I never did. Or never will. At least you'll be safe."

"I don't want to be safe—"

"Then you're crazy," he said with a snarl. "For once, why don't you stop trying to do the noble thing? Your lawyer is right to try to get you a plea deal." He was angry. It wasn't fair to take it out on her, but at the moment he didn't know how else to deal with it. All he saw was red. And fear. He was terrified.

"So, if I take the plea deal, you'll back down from going to prison in my place?"

"No. I'm still going through with this, but at least if you were considering a plea deal I'd know you hadn't completely lost your mind." He knew it was a damn harsh thing to say, but his wife needed to get some sense into her head. Doing the right thing was all well and good in most instances, but her life was on the line here. He needed to know she was ready to do whatever it took to save herself.

Her mouth dropped open. Silence. Then she curled her lip. "I haven't lost my mind. I'm not going to admit to a horrible crime I didn't commit. I'm not going to let every single person who doubted our marriage have the satisfaction of thinking they were right. I'm not going to disgrace the Prescott name. I'm innocent and I'm going to prove it."

"How?" he demanded. "What are you going to do? Leave the country and solve this?"

"Yes. I'll figure out who the thief is and clear my name," she said flatly. "And you can forget this crazy idea of going to prison on my behalf."

He sighed loudly. "If I get a plea deal of my own I'd be out in, what? Four or five years?"

"You'd destroy your family name. Nobody would want to do business with you. You'll be a pariah," she said desperately.

"So, what?" He shrugged. "You'll be safe. That's all that matters."

"What matters is that we do the right thing. Save Prescott from a thief. Clear my name."

"And if this goes to trial before we've caught the thief, you'll end up in prison for years," he said.

"Thirty years."

His heart sank like a stone. Weighed him down until he felt like he was falling into Hell. He clenched his fists. Allyson was not going to spend a day in prison. Not one day. "Last night, I thought I'd never see you again. You were locked away from me and I couldn't get to you. I'm never going to live with that ever again."

"I was the one locked up, remember?" Her eyes glistened. "It was horrible. I've never felt so trapped and alone in my whole life." Tears spilled down her cheeks and her body trembled. A strangled sob escaped her throat, and suddenly she was rushing across the room and wrapping herself around him on the sofa.

Dane held her so tightly he thought he might break her. Held her in his arms as she sat in his lap and sobbed. Listening to the sound of her anguished weeping was the most gut-wrenching, heart-rending moment of his life. He hadn't known it was possible to feel this much pain.

He smoothed a hand down over her dark hair and rocked back and forth, trying to comfort and soothe her. She clung to him desperately, each shuddering intake of breath stabbing him in the gut.

Finally, she pulled back and slipped out of his lap and onto the other side of the sofa. "I know you're trying to help me. But you have to let me do this the right way."

Before he could reply, his phone rang. Grabbing it from the coffee table, he quickly answered it. The familiar voice on the other end made his body go rigid. Her mother. More trouble.

He rubbed his eyes and leaned back in his seat. "Mrs. Smith? You're outside? Look, she's not in a good state right now—"

"Is that my mom?" Allyson asked.

He nodded.

"Let her in," his wife said.

"Allyson says she can see you," he said. When he ended the call he quickly contacted the concierge downstairs, asking him to let Allyson's mother up to their apartment.

After several minutes, Dane answered the knock on their front door.

Allyson's mother looked exhausted. He had contacted her last night after Allyson's arrest, and then to inform her that Allyson was home.

"Where is she?" Mrs. Smith swept into their apartment and found her daughter in the living room.

"Mom." Allyson rose to her feet and hugged her mother. "Where's Dad?"

Mrs. Smith sank into the sofa, the picture of distress. "He decided to stay with James and Holly at their place. Poor Holly was so worried about you, and she's so far along in her pregnancy. He wanted to stay behind to help her."

"Would you like something to eat?" Dane asked, shoving aside his annoyance at her mother flat-out ignoring him. She was probably in no state to remember he was even there.

Her mother waved her hand dismissively. "Later." It wasn't like her to seem so out of sorts. Usually she gushed whenever she came over to their luxury apartment.

"Mom, why didn't you tell us you were coming over?" Allyson asked.

"The truth is, dear, I've been wandering around the city, utterly despondent. We've been in town these last few weeks to take care of Holly, and now you've been carted off to jail. How could you do it?"

Allyson stared, taken aback. "Do what?"

"Steal? How could you steal all that money? It's all over the news. You walking out of jail. The whole city knows what you did," her mother said.

"You think I'm capable of such a thing?" His wife's hand flew to her chest, a horrified expression on her face.

"I know you probably didn't mean to cause any harm," her mother said. "But you have to give that money back. Save yourself from serious trouble."

"I didn't steal the money," Allyson said shrilly. "I would never do such a thing."

"A year ago, I would have believed that. But after you got your husband's company back I realize just how ruthless you really are," Mrs. Smith breathed.

Allyson gasped. "You think I'm a thief because I saved Prescott from the Handels?"

"I think you're more cunning and ruthless than you let on," her mother replied. "You'd have to be to survive as a rich man's wife."

He had heard just about enough. "You're not going to talk to this rich man's wife like that." He snarled at the words 'rich man's wife'.

Mrs. Smith stared at him, suddenly flustered. "I didn't mean any offense—"

"You've just accused my wife of being a thief," he said coldly. "You can either apologize to Allyson or you can get out."

"*Dane*," his wife cried.

"I mean it," he said through gritted teeth. "Say you're sorry, Mrs. Smith, or leave and never come back." Ordinarily he'd avoid talking to his mother-in-law like this, but nothing was off limits when it came to protecting and defending his wife. Not even throwing out his mother-in-law for good.

Mrs. Smith rose to her feet slowly, an outraged expression on her face. "I don't think I know you anymore. Either of you."

"So this should be easy for you," he said coldly. "Turn around and leave."

"Allyson?" Her mother cast her daughter a desperate glance.

"Just go, Mom," his wife murmured. "There's no talking to him when he gets like this. Dane means what he says. Just give us a chance to cool off. Please."

"Fine." His mother-in-law turned on her heel, stalked out of the living room and stormed out of the apartment, slamming the door behind her.

"She thinks I did this," Allyson said in disbelief. "My own mother thinks I'm capable of stealing money from my husband's company."

"Your mother has always been unfairly hard on you," he pointed out.

"Not like this," she said. "She used to pressure me to get married. Told me my job wasn't good enough. But she's never ever believed I could commit a crime. You heard what she said. A year ago, she wouldn't have believed this. But now she does. Everything has changed."

The truth was, his wife had been the one who'd had to do most of the adjusting when they got married. She was the one who'd had to enroll in college. Take etiquette lessons. Set up a whole new division at Prescott Global. Make friends with elites who would more than likely always be suspicious of her. And with these allegations coming out in the news, they'd be a hell of a lot more suspicious now.

Her entire life had been turned upside down. All because of him. All because he had pulled her into an upper-class life she hadn't been prepared for. "The only way to convince her otherwise is if I take the fall. If I go to prison instead of you," he said, trying to seize another opportunity to talk some sense into her.

"No. The only way to convince my mother is if I clear my name by figuring out who the real thief is," she said.

"We don't even know where the money is going," he reminded her.

"Then we have to figure that out," she said, "because I'm not letting this go. Doing the right thing means that neither of us has to go to jail."

"It means that if this goes to trial and goes badly, you'll end up in prison for thirty years," he said, desperation lacing every word. The thought of Allyson being locked up for that long made him sick to his stomach.

If he lost Allyson, all their dreams of a happy married life would die. They'd never have children. The house he had just bought would end up being a monument to their doomed love. A hideous reminder of his wife's imprisonment.

"Give me a chance," she pleaded. "Just one chance to solve this. Then, if we can't figure out who the thief is, we can revisit this."

It was the best she was going to give him. He was never going to let her go to prison. However, if giving her what she wanted for now could buy him some time to reason with her, he was willing to take it. "I'm going to call my father," he said stiffly. "Maybe he's finally figured out where the money is going."

She nodded. "I'll go get something to eat in the meantime."

As she headed into the kitchen, Dane reached for his cell phone. He got a hold of his father on the phone and together they started going over files, documents. Searched through their laptops until his father found something they'd all overlooked. Hidden. Almost so out in the open that it could be missed. But also buried deep enough to be flagged as off. He didn't think he could explain it to his wife. Yet it made sense. But there it was. A massive and unexplained amount of money moved into a bank account overseas.

He rushed into the kitchen. "I know where the money's going."

"Where?" Allyson asked from her seat at the kitchen island. "Should we go to the police with this?"

"Yes; we have no choice but to tell the cops," he said. "The money's being sent to London."

Her mouth fell open. "The Handels are in London."

"They run Prescott's London office," he said. "We'll be heading right into their territory."

His wife threw her shoulders back, a determined light flashing in her green eyes. "Then that's where we have to go. And so help them, if they're the ones doing this I'm going to hang them myself."

Chapter 9

The flight to London seemed to go on forever. Dane spent most of it holding his wife's hand, grateful he had access to a private jet. The flight would've felt even longer if they'd had to fly commercial.

After they touched down at Heathrow Airport, they got into one of the black cabs that London was famous for. They could have easily taken a private car, but Allyson wanted to travel in an authentic London cab.

The ride to the London Prescott Hotel seemed to last even longer than the flight. When they finally checked in to their luxury suite, his wife flopped down onto the huge king-sized bed.

Exhausted, he got into the bed beside her, too tired to even bother taking off his shoes. His father and Allyson's lawyer had flown in days earlier and were already staying at the hotel, but he was way too tired to go search them out right now.

"I can't believe I'm here. In London." The breathless excitement in her voice made him smile.

"We aren't here for a vacation," he reminded her.

"I know," she said, "but I've never been to Europe and now I'm here. I know it's for a bad reason, but I'm still going to make the most of this."

A week had gone by since she had gotten out of jail, and they had spent most of it making travel plans and trying to convince a judge to let Allyson leave the country. Dane knew that the judge had only agreed because of his family name. Outside of having the charges dropped, a Prescott could get a judge to do just about anything. At least, that's what his father had told him. The thought still made him queasy. How could anyone think Allyson would do something like stealing money?

If Allyson had been merely an employee at Prescott Global rather than the wife of the CEO, she wouldn't have been granted permission to fly to London. Hell, she probably wouldn't have had the money to make bail.

Still, she had been through a terrible ordeal with the allegations, and she deserved a little happiness.

He pulled her close and kissed the top of her head. The flowery, feminine scent of the shampoo she always used was intoxicating. Holding his beautiful wife in his arms was something he could never ever tire of. Especially now that he knew how easy it was to lose her. "You're the only person I know who could make the best of something so terrible," he murmured against her silky hair.

"Can you blame me?" she asked. "Our room is so beautiful."

He sat up to glance around, realizing that the huge suite hadn't even registered with him. Dane wasn't sure if that was because concern for his wife made him block out everything else, or if it was because he had taken his wealth for granted for so long that very little impressed him.

As he took in the room, he tried to see it from his wife's eyes: Gold and red brocade curtains, antique furniture, bookshelves lined with old leather-bound books, and genuine oil paintings on the walls that were covered with old-fashioned floral wallpaper. There was a stuffy sort of luxury to the suite. An old-fashioned elegance that was classically British.

"You know, I've never actually stayed here," he murmured.

"Really? Your parents own it," she said.

"I usually stay at one of my cousin's luxury apartments, but he sold the place and moved to Paris."

"Gosh, wouldn't it be lovely to live in Paris? Or here in London?" Her face lit up.

"I'd thought about moving out of New York City and settling down somewhere else." He chuckled, but it turned into something very tired and sad. "Back when our biggest problem was whether I wanted to stay on at Prescott."

"You should still think of things like that."

"You are my only concern," he said. "Nothing else matters now."

"I've ruined your life with this mess." She sighed. "You shouldn't have to worry about lawyers and jail sentences—"

"Neither should you," he interrupted. "I'm the one who dragged you into this life. I wanted to shower all this wealth on you, but I didn't see how dangerous all this could be."

She sat up, tucking her legs under her. "You didn't drag me, Dane. You've given me the most beautiful life a woman could ask for. These past six months have been the best months of my whole life."

"And now that's over," he muttered.

"No." She placed a hand on his cheek. The touch of her fingertips made him want to pull her into his arms and kiss away all her pain and fear. A single touch from her was all it took to turn him into a man he barely recognized. A focused, ruthless animal who would do anything to protect what was his. Her.

"No, it's not over," she continued. "I'd rather be fighting this right now with you than be free of this without you. Don't you see? The worst day of my life with you will always be better than the best day without you."

Damn, he loved her. Loved her so much it was going to destroy him. Because he would tear this whole city apart to save her. Tear it apart and crush whoever had caused this to happen to her. And if they didn't figure out who had done this, he would go to prison in her place. Let her think that he was giving her the chance to clear her name. Let her think he'd accept her case going to trial. Let her think he'd allow her to risk thirty years in prison.

It was wrong to lie to his wife. Wrong to let her think he was accepting her stubborn desire for justice, but Dane didn't give a damn. The only thing worse than lying to his wife was letting her spend the next thirty years of her life behind bars.

For now, he'd help her find evidence to clear her name. If that didn't work, he was ready to go to prison in her place.

"That's pretty grim, no matter how you slice it," he said finally.

She pressed her mouth to his, the sensation of her soft lips on his making him groan.

When she pulled away, she said softly, "Every day with you is the best day."

"You sure you're going to be saying that tomorrow?" he asked with a raised eyebrow.

Allyson took a deep breath. "As bad as tomorrow is going to be, I'll get through it if you're with me."

He lay back down on the bed, pulling her down with him. "As long as you're ready to take on the Handels."

THERE WAS SOMETHING intimidating about the Prescott Tower in downtown London. It was dark, shooting straight up into the sky. The weather held an ominous feel to it, making the grey concrete of the tower even more menacing against the vintage buildings surrounding it.

Allyson let her husband help her out of their rented luxury car. She shivered. It was probably the gray autumn morning that was making her cold, but there was something foreboding about the tower. From where she stood in the shadow of the tower, it looked like it was made of black glass. *Like the London Tower, where many innocent people were tortured, or killed.* She shivered again. *Bad comparison.*

"Isn't it magnificent?" Dane's father, Alfred, asked as he stepped out of the car and walked over to her.

She frowned. "If you say so."

"The building's new," Alfred said. "I remember it during the construction phase. Now look at it. One of the tallest buildings in London."

Their New York office was taller, but this place still intimidated her. Reminded her that this wasn't a gleaming, modern, hopeful-looking place like Prescott headquarters in New York City. This was the Handels' turf, and the cold design of the building made that unmistakable.

Dane headed into the lobby and she followed him with Alfred, his assistant Fran, and her lawyer Lester Crane bringing up the rear. They were guided into a conference room, a huge dark table taking up the center of the room.

Her eyes fell on Nicholas Handel sitting at the head of the table, his sister Katherine standing guard behind the large chair.

"Ah, right on time." The corners of Nicholas' mouth curved upward in a smile that didn't reach his dark eyes.

Allyson hated having to do this. Hated having to come to the Handels' turf and ask for a favor. Luckily, her lawyer was here to soften the blow, but it still bothered her. Still felt as if, after she had defeated the Handel siblings, she now had to admit her own defeat.

Keeping her head held high, she forced herself to return Nicky's smile.

Nicky gestured to the seats at the table. "Please, everyone have a seat. What can I get you all? Coffee? Tea?"

"Coffee and tea would be fine, thank you," Fran piped up.

Nicholas grinned at Fran. "I see Prescott has hired another lovely assistant."

Fran blushed, and eagerly took a seat by Nick's side.

With a roll of her eyes, Allyson sat down between Dane and her lawyer. She had decided to let her assistant, Cameron, stay behind in

New York; with Alfred still recovering from a heart attack, having an assistant like Fran around was for the best.

Ordinarily she wouldn't have wanted her father-in-law to make such a long trip to London, but Alfred understood finances like nobody else. If the thief really was in London, they would need Alfred's expertise.

Soon, refreshments were served. Lester started informing Nicholas and Katherine about the embezzlement case.

"And here I thought you had all come to London to gloat," Nicholas said once Lester was finished.

"You're both still working at Prescott," Allyson pointed out. "That should be proof enough that there are no hard feelings on our end."

"Oh, please," Katherine snapped. "The only reason you kept us on was as a favor to my father."

Katherine wasn't exactly wrong. Her father, John Handel, had helped push his children out of the New York office months ago, but he still wanted Nicholas and Katherine to stay on at the London office. As much as John Handel had wanted to teach his children a lesson he just wasn't the cutthroat type, and didn't have the heart to cut them off completely.

Which meant trouble for Allyson's plans. If the Handel siblings were angry enough to prevent her from looking at files in the London office, that would be one less chance at solving this mystery.

Allyson took a sip of her coffee to calm her nerves. "I admire your father and everything he's done. It's obvious that he still cares about both of you."

"Shouldn't you be behind bars anyway?" Katherine sniffed derisively.

"We're here to clear my client's name," Lester cut in. "Access to some of your files would be valuable to our investigation."

"And what's in it for us?" Katherine demanded.

"We won't accuse you of helping the embezzler," Dane said coldly.

She cast her husband a warning glance. Even now, he couldn't keep his disdain inside. When it came to protecting her, Dane could never listen to reason. Could never just play along. The truth was, he wasn't that type of man. He would never grovel or beg or play nice. It just wasn't in his nature, but she hoped her warning glance got him to rein in some of his impulsiveness.

"You really think the thief is in this office?" Nicholas leaned forward, a pensive expression on his face.

"It makes sense," Allyson said. "We know that Prescott's money is being sent and probably laundered to London. The most logical place for that kind of activity would be Prescott's London office."

Katherine glared at Allyson. "So, if we help you clear your name, you won't drag us down with you. I really underestimated you. I thought you were this simpering Yank but you're an iron fist in a velvet glove, aren't you?"

Her words reminded Allyson of her mother's suspicion. Her own mother hadn't trusted her. Had actually believed she was capable of stealing millions of dollars from Prescott Global. Called her cunning and ruthless.

Now it seemed Katherine believed that, too. Months ago, Allyson would have worn that with some amount of pride, but now it just made her sick to her stomach. The world actually believed that she was an unscrupulous thief, who deserved to go to prison.

"My client is merely trying to clear her name," Lester said. "Do we have permission to access the files?"

Nicky scoffed. "We all know Dane has the power to overrule whatever we say. He's the company CEO, after all."

"We thought it was better to ask, rather than just muscle our way in," Allyson said softly.

Rising to his feet, Nicholas gave her a hard stare. "You're welcome to access our files, but first I thought we should give you a grand tour of our new offices."

Katherine gasped. "You're just going to hand over sensitive information like that?"

"We have nothing to hide," Nicholas said to his sister.

Katherine scowled, but said nothing.

"I think taking a tour is a suitable exchange," Lester murmured.

"Brilliant." Nicholas grinned, and gestured to the door of the conference room. "Shall we start the tour?"

Allyson swallowed hard, knowing they had very little choice. Sure, they could force the Handels to hand over the files, but this was their territory. They knew the place inside and out, which meant the Handel siblings had the advantage.

She nodded, and they all followed Nicholas out of the conference room. Nicholas introduced them to senior staff members, and showed them art from upcoming advertising campaigns. Finally, he stopped to introduce them to the manager of the women's department.

"This is Rebecca Greene," Nicholas said, introducing a young woman sporting glasses and a designer pantsuit.

Allyson regarded Rebecca warily. The money was being funneled out of this division at company headquarters. It made sense for her counterpart at the London office to be a prime suspect. Making a mental note to look further into Rebecca's work in the women's department, Allyson reached out to briefly shake Rebecca's hand. "Nice to meet you, Ms. Greene," she said.

"Pleasure," Rebecca said with a smile. "It's an honor to meet you, Mrs. Prescott. After all, I wouldn't have a job here if you hadn't created a whole new division in New York."

"Allyson, it would be really beneficial if you and Rebecca could work together on the new football line," Nicholas interrupted. "We've been planning to get more girls into football across the country, and making sure the equipment is suitable for them. We're talking American football here, not our English footy."

"I'd seen some of the plans about that," Allyson said, ignoring the comment on American vs. British football. She might not be athletic, but she worked for a sports company that was international; she knew the difference. It was her job to know it. "I'd love to work with Rebecca."

"Wonderful," Nicky said. "Listen, we're having a work do at my flat later this week. You two could chat then and exchange ideas for the football initiative."

"Oh, thank you for the invitation," Allyson said.

"Absolutely. You're all invited," Nicholas replied. "I'll ring you later with the details."

After the tour ended, Nicholas retrieved some files and handed a box full of them over to Lester. "Here you are, old man."

Lester raised an eyebrow. "Thank you. I'll have these returned to you as soon as possible."

With that, they said their goodbyes and headed back to their car for the drive back to the London Prescott Hotel.

Walking hand in hand with her husband, she headed up to their floor of the hotel. As scared as she was, having Dane so close made her feel stronger. Somehow, they had gotten some files from the Handels. She had no idea if they would be much help, but at least there was hopefully something they didn't previously have.

Dane unlocked the door to their luxury suite and she stepped inside. A small white piece of paper on the carpet caught her eye. Bending over, she picked it up and stared at the handwriting. Her stomach lurched as she read the words scrawled on the paper:

Leave London and never come back.

Chapter 10

"What's that?" Dane looked over her shoulder at the threatening note, anger already simmering inside him. "What the hell!"

His wife's face had paled, and she rushed over to the sitting area to sit down. "I...I don't know. It was on the floor. Do you think it's a joke?"

He shook his head.

"Who could have written something like this?"

He headed over to the mini bar and poured out two glasses of scotch. When he walked over to the sitting area, he handed Allyson a glass and motioned for her to drink.

She emptied the glass of scotch so quickly he doubted she needed any prompting. "This is a nightmare," she gasped out. She looked near tears, or like she was hitting a breaking point. It drove Dane mad; his wife had always been someone in control when he worked as his assistant. The past months had been too much. And now this... what were they going to do?

"I'll call security," he said, taking a seat across from her. He reached for his phone, got the hotel's security chief on the line, and explained the situation.

"I'm looking through security footage from today, Mr. Prescott, and I'm not seeing anything out of the ordinary," the security chief said. "I see your father and your lawyer heading inside with an assistant. Then I see them coming outside with you and your wife a few minutes later."

Dane narrowed his eyes. "And that's all?"

"Well, there's the cleaning staff as well. Shall I investigate this further with your room's maid, sir?" the security officer asked.

"You think the cleaning staff is capable of leaving a note like this?" Dane asked. "Could they have been paid by someone to drop off the note?" Allyson's hands shot up and she shook her head forcefully. "No, Dane. I don't want to get anyone on the cleaning staff in trouble. Let's just leave it alone. Whoever it was, it wouldn't be them."

He hated the idea of someone threatening them, but his wife would never forgive him if someone on staff lost their job. "Please just ask. If someone looks suspicious or guilty, please let us know. Otherwise, leave it. We'll figure this out. It's probably just a mistake anyway." Dane hung up and focused his attention back on Allyson.

"It's probably nothing," she said. Despite her words, she looked shaken.

"It doesn't sound like nothing."

She blew out a ragged breath. "It must be a prank. We're around the right kind of people who would do something like this."

"This sounds like the kind of petty, vindictive stunt Katherine Handel would make," he muttered.

"That would explain why Nicholas was so ready to invite us to his apartment." She rubbed her temples. "Katherine and Nicholas are probably toying with us by trying to scare us with the note. It wouldn't surprise me if they invited us over just to see our reaction."

He frowned. "But how could they have gotten the note into the room?"

"You know Katherine," she said. "She knew we were coming to her office today; she could have easily paid one of the maids to slip the note inside while we were out."

Anger made him ball up his fists. The Handels were always up to something. They never played fair, and fought back when threatened. After Allyson managed to beat them at their own game and send them packing back to London, they were probably doing whatever they could to get their revenge. This note was likely the start of it. And if their past behavior was anything to go by, they had a hand in more than just sending threatening notes. "What if the Handels set up the embezzlement and are trying to scare us off their trail?"

"I can't imagine them being thieves. How could they have been embezzling while they were in America? Wouldn't they have said something? They'd have been stealing from their own company. That doesn't make sense. But I guess we have to look at every possibility." She sighed. "What on earth could their motive be?"

"Revenge," he said. "Maybe this mess hasn't been about money at all. Maybe it's been a frame job to ruin you."

"Dammit," she breathed. "That does sound like something they would do. I doubt they'd ever have a reason to steal, but they'd probably do anything to try to destroy us and the company now."

"We have the files they gave us," he said. "If they're trying to set us up, maybe the files won't be as helpful as we'd like."

She sighed. "I think we have to go talk to Lester."

After sending a text to Lester, letting him know they were heading over to his suite, Dane escorted his wife to her lawyer's room.

Lester showed them into the sitting area of his room. The table and chairs were already covered with documents and folders.

Quickly, Allyson filled Lester in on the note and their suspicions of the Handel siblings.

"I've read up on this Nicholas Handel," Lester said, sitting down and gesturing for them to sit down as well. "He's brilliant. Very good at what he does, but a real nasty piece of work. His sister is probably even more brilliant and even nastier than he is."

"Have you discovered anything in the files they handed over?" Dane took a seat beside his wife.

"I might have," Lester said. "But it might also be insignificant."

"What is it?" Allyson asked.

"I've gone over some of the files, and there's one very large sum of money that stood out to me," Lester replied. "It's a trust fund that holds the exact amount of money that has gone missing from Prescott. And the fund has been set up for one of Nicholas Handel's heirs."

Dane scratched his jaw. "I don't remember Nicholas Handel having any heirs."

"Unless his sister Katherine counts as an heir," his wife suggested.

"That's just it," Lester said. "This kind of trust only gets set up by a certain type of kin. A wife or a child, for instance. People who are considered dependents. Katherine couldn't be his heir. Neither could his parents."

She scoffed. "Nicholas definitely isn't married, and I doubt he has a kid."

"Are you sure about that?" Lester asked with a raised eyebrow.

"I'm pretty sure the tabloids would have gotten wind of something like that," she said. "The London press is obsessed with the Handels, especially now that they're back in England."

"Well, regardless of what the tabloids say, Nicholas Handel has an heir," Lester said. "And that heir has a trust that's the exact amount that has gone missing from Prescott Global."

"Why would Nicholas give you a document like that if he was trying to hide it?" Dane asked.

"He isn't. Not really. Nicholas might be trying to hide the fact that he has an heir, but there's no way he knows about this trust fund," Lester said. "If he did, he never would have handed over such a document."

"So, if his heir is the thief, and the thief has set up an independent trust fund with stolen money, Nicholas has no idea," Allyson said, sounding amazed.

"Katherine Handel might know, though," Dane said.

"It's possible, since she wasn't the one who gave me the box of documents. Nicholas did that," Lester said.

"Not to mention Katherine wasn't exactly thrilled about having to hand over the files to us," his wife reminded them.

No, she hadn't been. And if Dane was remembering correctly, Katherine had been downright hostile. The idea of her brother handing over all those documents had really riled her up. At the time he had thought it was Katherine's typically combative nature, but there was also a chance that she was up to something.

Dane leaned forward in his seat. "What's the plan now, Crane?"

Lester reached for a folder and started looking through it. "The only way to figure this out is to talk to the heir."

His wife chewed her lower lip thoughtfully. "Is there any clue in that file about who Nicky's heir could be?"

"No clues at all, unfortunately," Lester said grimly. "At this point it looks like the heir's existence and identity are a closely-guarded secret. There's proof of some kind lying around, but we don't have that kind of access. Not without a warrant. And we can't get a warrant with so little to go on."

"Don't tell me this is a dead end," Dane said. He hated that his wife seemed hell-bent on clearing her name rather than allowing him to go to prison for her, but the idea of admitting defeat to the Handels didn't sit well with him.

"It doesn't have to be," Allyson said. "If we went to the police and they got a warrant...where would we want them to search?"

Lester furrowed his brow. "The Prescott Tower and any Handel residences, I'd imagine."

"That's what I thought," she said softly. "We've been invited to Nicky's apartment later this week."

He didn't like that determined look in her eyes. "No. I forbid it," Dane said flatly.

"You haven't even heard my idea yet," she countered defiantly.

"There's no way in hell I'm letting you sneak around that man's house," Dane forced out. "That's just asking for trouble." She'd been in enough trouble. He wasn't about to let her risk being arrested in another country. He couldn't pull strings back in New York; it was going to be even worse here.

"I have to agree with your husband, Mrs. Prescott," Lester said. "Sneaking around and stealing documents would be highly unethical. Not to mention illegal."

"Who said anything about stealing?" she asked. "I could just take photos of whatever evidence I find. It's not a crime to take photos in a apartment you've been invited to."

Dane stared at his wife, totally stunned. "You've been working in corporate America for too long."

"Oh, come on," she said. "We came to London to clear my name. So, let's clear it."

He crossed his arms. "What happens if you get caught sneaking around and you end up getting arrested again?"

"I'll have you to help me so that doesn't happen," she said breezily.

It irked him that she didn't seem to be taking the consequences of her insane idea seriously. "How exactly do you expect me to help you with this mad scheme?"

"You and Mr. Crane can distract everyone while I look through the house," she replied. "Nicholas is bound to have a study or a home office. I bet that's where he keeps his important documents."

"As potentially dangerous as that sounds, it could help with our case," Lester said.

Dane narrowed his eyes at the lawyer. "Are you kidding me? A second ago you were talking about how unethical all this was."

"That's when I thought Mrs. Prescott would be stealing evidence," Lester said. "Taking photos really isn't all that criminal."

He glanced at his wife and their eyes met. The determination hadn't left her face. "There's no talking you out of this, is there?"

She shook her head. "No. My own mother believes I'm a thief. This isn't just about clearing my name. It's about getting my family to trust and believe in me again. I need this, Dane. I need us to at least try."

With a heavy sigh, he said, "Fine. We'll do this. But you have to promise you won't tell my father or drag him into this plan."

"I promise I won't," she assured him.

The determined expression on her face shifted to one of relief. A relief he didn't share. Because if there was one thing Dane trusted it was his gut. And his gut told him the worst was yet to come.

BUCKINGHAM PALACE LOOMED in front of them. Allyson squeezed her way through the crowd and pressed up right against the black front gate. Her phone was out, and she held it up to take some shots.

There was a slight chill in the autumn air, but she didn't mind. Seeing all the London sights today had been totally worth it. The expansive palace was stately, full of windows that the public couldn't see into. But the flag wasn't flying at full mast, so the queen wasn't in residence; still, she felt a jolt of excitement.

When she finally got the shots she wanted, she squeezed back through the crowd and found Dane.

"Ready to go to the park?" he asked.

She nodded excitedly, and together they walked arm in arm to St. James's Park. The park was beautiful now that the leaves had changed color. The autumn foliage had turned into brilliant shades of vivid red and stunning gold.

After they walked lazily through the park they made their way to a nearby fish and chip shop, with Allyson settling into a booth and Dane going up front to make their order.

Finally, he arrived with their orders

"It's so warm and cozy here." She popped a warm fried potato chip into her mouth.

"Did you enjoy the tour of the city?" Dane asked, cutting into his fish.

She nodded excitedly. In addition to seeing Buckingham Palace, they had visited the wax museum and visited Big Ben. It was all very cheesy tourist stuff rather than the fancy things she was still adjusting to, but with the stress of everything she needed to do something fun. Something that took her mind off the fact that later tonight they'd be sneaking around Nicholas Handel's London apartment.

Which was easier said than done. Right now, her lawyer was probably on a video conference call with the prosecutor of her embezzlement case. She didn't like it since there might be a plea deal involved, but she could easily shoot it down. If they got enough evidence to clear her name tonight, they wouldn't need a plea deal.

The thoughts going around her head didn't exactly help to steady her nerves.

Dane reached across the table to squeeze her hand gently. "Your lawyer knows what he's doing."

"I know that," she said. "Crane is a great attorney, but I don't like the idea of a plea deal."

He sighed. "Neither do I. Which is why I still want to take the fall for all of this."

She groaned inwardly. Her husband still hadn't let that go. Dane really thought the best way to deal with all this was to admit to something he didn't do. The only thing worse than everyone thinking she was a thief was Dane going to prison in her place for something he didn't do. "I'm not discussing this again."

"Tough, because we *are* going to discuss it," he said. "There's no way in hell you're going to talk me out of this. It's the best plan and you know it."

Before she could come up with a retort, her phone rang loudly. She fished into her handbag and retrieved it. Seeing that it was Lester, she quickly answered it. "Hello?"

"Hi, Mrs. Prescott," Lester said. "I've just wrapped things up with the prosecution."

Apprehension made her heart hammer wildly. "Yes? What did they say?"

"Well, I think it's good news, though you might not see it that way," Lester replied. "The prosecution is willing to give you a plea deal. You plead guilty and get three years, instead of risking a trial."

She bit her lip. "I see."

"Here's the thing, though—we don't have long to decide. The plea deal is only on the table for a short amount of time," he went on.

"How long do we have?" she asked.

Her lawyer's next words filled her with dread. "We have to get back to the States as soon as possible. The plea deal is only on the table for the next four days."

Chapter 11

Her eyes looked haunted. Like she had seen a ghost and heard the worst news of her life all at the same time. He wished he could take her away from all this and head down to the Bahamas. To their villa where they'd gotten married. Where everything had been safe, and perfect. He wanted the light back in her eyes. This was all his fault.

When Allyson hung up her phone, he asked, "What is it?"

"That was Lester," she replied softly.

He clenched his jaw, bracing himself for the bad news. "Has he finished speaking with the prosecutor?"

She nodded. "He's negotiated a plea deal. But I have to decide and get back to the States within four days."

"You're not going to take it," he said firmly. "We're going to call Lester back right now and make him pin this on me. We'll say I put you up to taking the fall, but I changed my mind and have decided to turn myself in."

"No. You're not going to jail for me," she said.

Crossing his arms, he narrowed his eyes at his wife. Damn her stubbornness. Damn her unwillingness to listen to reason. "Stop being noble. Put Lester back on the phone."

"No."

"That's not a suggestion, Allyson," he said flatly. "If you won't call him back, I will."

"I'm not letting you sit in prison for three years for something you didn't do," she said.

"Ditto," he said.

"I'm the one who's been accused," she said. "Not you."

"So, you're taking the deal?" he asked.

"No, I'm not," she said. "We've been over this. I'm not admitting to something I didn't do. I'm not going to disgrace my family like this. I refuse to let the world go on thinking I'm this dishonest person."

"Better to be free with everyone thinking you're guilty than to be locked up and everyone thinking you're innocent," he said harshly. "Listen to reason. You won't let me go in your place. You refuse to take a plea deal with a reduced sentence. This insanity has gone on long enough."

She inhaled sharply, her eyes shining with tears. "You have no idea what this is like. To have your own mother look at you like she doesn't know you. I can't live with that. I won't."

"I beg you," he ground out, "don't do this. Don't force me to go on without you for thirty years. I can't do that. If you go away, Allyson, you might as well kill me. Because I can't live without you."

Allyson covered her face with her hands, but he could hear her softly sobbing. Her shoulders heaved like the weight of the world was breaking her apart.

The sight of his wife in so much distress tore at his heart. Filled him with an agony he couldn't begin to describe. The desperation that gripped him now was driving him so insane he couldn't breathe. His chest constricted painfully. The thought of losing her. Of watching her go to prison for decades. It was almost like finding out she was dying.

"Give me tonight," she said, her voice hitching.

"What?"

"Let me look for the evidence at Nicky's apartment." She lowered her hands, revealing a wan face streaked with tears. The sight tore at his heart all over again. "Let me try to find evidence that clears my name. Who knows? If I find something good enough, maybe things won't even have to go to trial. Maybe they'll drop these charges entirely and get the real thief."

"If I give you tonight, will you promise to let me go to prison in your place if you don't find anything?" he asked.

She nodded solemnly. "I promise. I'll let you go ahead with your plan."

He slumped back in his chair, relief coursing through him. But the relief suddenly gave way to another worry. Allyson's promise made tonight even more dangerous than he had anticipated.

The prospect of him going to jail in her place could make his wife do something reckless and dangerous just to keep him out of jail. Because, as different as they were from each other, they were both alike in one way. There was nothing either of them wouldn't do to protect the other. And if Dane was willing to give his life to protect his wife, there was no telling what Allyson might to do save him.

"Just don't do anything crazy tonight," he said. "Don't take any unnecessary risks."

"I won't," she promised.

Allyson was always honest with him, so somehow his wife's word was going to have to be enough.

SHE HADN'T HAD JITTERS about getting dressed since her wedding day. Yet Allyson was a bundle of nerves as slipped into the short blue cocktail dress.

"You look beautiful," Dane said behind her. He whistled. "Damn sexy. Maybe we should just stay here."

Turning away from the mirror to look at him, she forced a smile. Her husband looked so handsome in the light gray suit he was wearing. He wasn't wearing a tie, making his formal outfit look less formal and slightly dangerous. "Thank you. You look very handsome."

He walked up to her and took her hands in his. "You remember what we discussed?"

She nodded, remembering the plan they had gone over in the fish and chip shop earlier today. Dane would distract Katherine and Nicholas by suggesting some business venture that they couldn't resist.

Meanwhile she would talk business with Rebecca Greene, and then slip away from the conversation long enough to snoop around.

"Yes, I do," she breathed.

Suddenly Dane cupped her face in his hands. His touch made her body tingle all over. What she wouldn't give to forget about their troubles and spend the rest of the night in bed with her husband. His blue eyes burned into hers, reminding her that she was his.

Desperate for more contact she leaned forward, grabbed the lapels of his jacket, and pressed her mouth to his. Heat unfurled in her stomach, spreading through her entire body. All she was now was wanton longing.

His hands slid away from her face and he grasped the nape of her neck possessively. She already had her lipstick on, but she didn't care. Let him kiss it off. Let him kiss away all the pain and fear and torment.

He pried open her mouth with his tongue and she took him in, her tongue meeting his. As their tongues collided she clung to him even more tightly, not wanting this moment with the man she loved to ever end. She needed this. Needed him. Needed his touch. His body.

Better to get lost in the sensation their bodies gave each other than to let him see the truth in her eyes. She had lied to him. Made a promise she had no intention of keeping. If he knew what she was planning, her husband would never forgive her. But at least he would be free.

Free to live. To work. To find love again if he wanted it. That thought made her pull away abruptly. She couldn't kiss him with the thought of him moving on to another woman flashing in her head.

He rested his forehead on hers. "Be careful tonight."

"I will." That was another lie. Tonight, she had no intention of being careful.

Pulling away from him, she turned her attention back to the mirror. She reapplied her makeup and slipped into her cashmere coat.

Then, she and Dane stepped out of their suite and met up with Lester, Alfred, and Alfred's assistant to take the rented luxury car to Nicholas Handel's apartment.

Nicholas greeted them at the door and offered to take them on a tour of the luxury apartment. The space was expansive, pristine. There were scores of guests, Prescott's London staff as well as London's elite mingling, sipping drinks, and eating oysters. It was all very decadent, a show of Nicky's power and influence despite the fact that Alfred, Prescott's founder, and Dane, Prescott's CEO, were senior to him.

Just as Allyson had suspected there was an office, and she knew that she was going to have to sneak back there unnoticed sometime during the night.

After the tour, Dane started talking to Nicholas and Katherine. Allyson made sure to keep them in her sights as she approached Rebecca Greene on the far side of the living room.

"You look lovely, Rebecca," Allyson said.

Rebecca beamed. She was sporting a black lace knee-length dress that fit her beautifully. "Thank you, Mrs. Prescott. So do you. You look very elegant tonight."

"Thank you." Allyson smiled. She hated wondering if a perfectly nice woman like Rebecca was the one responsible for the embezzlement. It seemed so unlikely, but anything was possible now.

As they talked about work and the girl's football line that Nicholas had suggested, Allyson felt her insides knot up. The moment of truth was approaching, and she was on edge.

"I hate to ask, but do you would you happen to have a tampon or anything?" Allyson interrupted, her face turning bright red. She could feel the burn on her cheeks and all the way down her neck. It was the perfect cover- up.

"Oh, you're in luck." Rebecca reached into her tiny clutch and discreetly handed a tampon to Allyson. "I've got some painkillers as well if you need any."

"That's all right, thank you," Allyson said. "I'll just head over to the bathroom."

She hurried away from Rebecca and stepped out of the living room. Making her way down the hall, she looked over her shoulder to make sure nobody was around. She rushed by the bathroom and slipped into Nicky's office, gently closing the door behind her.

The office was dark except for the light of the moon streaming in through the window. Turning on the light would probably make her search easier, but she didn't want to risk anyone seeing the glow of the light from outside.

Her heart hammered in her chest. Sweat formed on her brow. Steeling herself, she walked over to the large desk in front of the bookcase and opened the top drawer. She retrieved her phone from her purse to use it as a flashlight while she rifled through the documents in the drawer.

There were financial statements, memos, business plans. Nothing that seemed helpful. Frustrated, she turned her attention to the other drawers. There were more documents. Contracts, business letters, legal filings. A manila folder that was stamped with the word 'Confidential' caught her attention. With her hands shaking, she reached into the folder and pulled out the contents.

She gasped as she held her phone over the words to read. Nicholas Handel's will. A will that bequeathed most of his fortune to charities, but with one small exception.

Suddenly the sound of approaching footsteps made her jerk in surprise. Her heart jumped into her throat. As fast as she could, she shoved her phone back into her purse.

The doorknob on the office door rattled.

Oh shit. Someone was trying to get in. If it was Nicholas, she was done for. She had no way of explaining her presence in his office. Realizing there was no time to put the documents back properly, her eyes darted around the room for a hiding place.

She was having a hard time adjusting to the near darkness of the room. Ducking under the table seemed like a bad idea, but then, in the light of the moon, she spotted the huge velvet curtain that had been pulled back from the window.

The door began to creak open. With her heart slamming against her ribs she scurried behind the heavy curtain, hoping to God that nobody found her.

Footsteps sounded as someone stepped into the room.

Please don't turn on the light. Please don't turn on the light.

She held her breath, her hands still gripping the documents in her hand. The terror of making a sound that gave her away was almost unbearable.

Another set of footsteps.

"*Nicholas.*" Dane's voice. He sounded agitated. "Forget about the book. My father wants to talk to you about this investment I was telling you about."

"Suit yourself," Nicholas said. "But then I win the bet. I have the book here."

"Fine." Dane gave out an exasperated breath. "You know how it is with fathers."

Nicholas snorted. "Tell me about it."

The sound of door creaking shut made her exhale, desperate to catch her breath. The sound of the footsteps began to fade, and she slipped out from behind the curtain.

She knew Nicholas Handel's secret now. Knew what he was hiding. And if there was time, there could very well be a chance to solve the mystery. Figure out who the embezzler was. But there was no time. Dane had given her a firm demand.

He'd given her the chance to sneak around Nicky's home with the assurance that, if she didn't get enough evidence to clear her name, he'd go to jail in her place. She had promised to let him go ahead with that plan. But she had no intention of keeping that promise.

Allyson folded the documents in her hand and shoved them into her purse. Stealing something this valuable was a huge risk, but she needed to have a backup plan in case things went awry.

With the documents now in her purse, she raced out of the office and locked herself in the bathroom. Tears stung her eyes. She stared at her reflection in the mirror. The face staring back at her looked exhausted. Ghostly pale.

"Get it together," she hissed at her reflection.

Fighting back tears, she squared her shoulders. She had no intention of letting her husband go to jail in her place. The only way to save Dane was to agree to the terms of the plea deal. Admit to a crime she didn't commit and face three years in prison. The thought of the whole world thinking she was a thief made her heart ache. But the thought of Dane in prison because of her was something she could never live with. Ever.

Taking a deep breath, she stepped out of the bathroom, ready to lie to her husband for the second time since they had gotten married.

Chapter 12

That had been close. Too close.

He walked with Nicholas down the hall and back out into the living room. Dane could have sworn he saw Allyson head towards the office, which was why he had tried to stop Nicholas from walking in. It had been too dark to see inside the office, so there was a chance his wife was still inside.

He wasn't going to take any chances. When he and Nicholas found his father and Katherine talking in a corner, he made a point to give them as much financial advice as possible.

Allyson appeared by his side minutes later. She touched his arm and motioned for him to follow her.

"Excuse us for a second," he said to his father and the Handel siblings.

"Of course," Nicholas said with a nod.

Dane followed Allyson out onto the balcony.

"Did you find anything?" he whispered into her ear.

She nodded and then lowered her eyes. Something was wrong. Her entire demeanor was off. His wife's face was pale. Her entire body tensed. "I figured out what sort of heir Nicholas has."

"Wife or kid?" he asked.

"He has a secret wife," she said. "Based on the date in his will, they haven't been married very long. However, he isn't leaving her that much money."

That didn't surprise him. Nicholas was selfish and stingy. Or maybe his wife already had plenty of money of her own.

"Did the will say who his wife was?" he pressed.

"No," she replied. "But I have my suspicions. Rebecca Greene is at the top of the list."

"That makes sense," he said. "She's in charge of the women's department at the London office. She would have access to accounts from headquarters. A scheme like that would be much harder for her to pull off from London, but not impossible."

"Do you think we should wait this out?" she asked. "Try to get more evidence?"

He shook his head. "There isn't enough time. We need to talk to your lawyer, and get my lawyer on the phone right now. Get them to get the charges applied to me."

"We should probably get out of here and hash things out with Lester." She sighed, her entire body shuddering.

Dane reached for her and pulled her close. Held her tightly to him. The warmth of her soft body against his tempted him more than anything ever had. If this was going to be one of their last nights together, he wanted to hold her in his arms for as long as possible.

When they finally pulled away from each other, Allyson headed back into the living room to find Lester while he went over to his father.

Somehow, they managed to get out of the party early after saying goodbye to the Handel siblings, and they went back to the hotel.

Lester met them in their suite while Dane got his lawyer on the phone.

"Mr. Prescott, I cannot advise you to do this," his lawyer, Jack Strickland, said. "I understand that you want to protect your wife, but admitting to a crime you didn't commit will come with serious consequences."

"I don't want your advice," Dane barked. "Just do as I say."

"It's pretty early in the morning over here, but I should be able to get the prosecutor on the phone," his lawyer replied.

"Do it," Dane muttered.

As the night wore on they hashed out a deal with Dane's lawyer, finally getting the charges moved to Dane. "This only works if you're back in New York by next Tuesday afternoon."

That was a little less than four days. Perfectly doable. If he could find a way to say goodbye to Allyson. "What happens after I meet up with you?" Dane asked his lawyer.

"Well, you'll be taken into custody. After that you'll be sentenced and start serving a three-year sentence," Jack replied. "Are you sure this is something you want?"

"It is," he said determinedly. "My wife is not going to jail."

With everything settled, Dane finished up some of the finer details with his lawyer on the phone while Allyson made final preparations with Lester.

"You don't have to do this," Allyson said, appearing beside him after showing Lester out of their suite.

"It's the only way," he said. "I could never accept you going away for even a minute. The night you spent in jail is not something I ever want you relive again."

Her lower lip trembled, and her shoulders slumped in defeat. "Oh, Dane. This is ridiculous. We'll get this sorted. We'll find out what's going on. We'll find a way."

"Will you wait for me?" he asked. "Three years is a long time."

"I'd wait forever for you." She inhaled sharply, like she was trying to stifle a sob.

Seeing her like this was destroying him. He crossed over to her and wrapped his arms around her tightly. She clung to him.

Without even thinking, his lips took hers in an aching, desperate kiss. This might be the last real night they spent together for three years. Tomorrow he'd get on a plane and head back to New York, where he'd undoubtedly spend most of his final free days working with his lawyer.

He had to have her one last time. Had to remember every inch of her perfect body.

Dane pulled away from her to lift her into his arms, walked her over to the bed, and set her down gently.

"I want you," he said gruffly, already ripping off his jacket.

The moment he said the words his wife tugged off her cocktail dress, down to nothing but a pair of high heels and lacy red underwear. "And I want you."

"You are the most beautiful thing I've ever seen," he choked out. Drinking her in made his heart slam hard in his chest. He was almost insane with desire for her, painfully hard. Needing to get out of the rest of his clothes he tossed them off until he was down to nothing, his erection pointing right at her.

Her skin was flushed, her full breasts heaving as she breathed. Slowly she pulled off her red lace panties, the explicit sight of her sex drowning out every coherent thought in his head. When she licked her lips provocatively, whatever it was that was holding him back snapped. Dane climbed onto the bed and took her mouth with his again.

Allyson arched her back as he rolled on top of her. With their tongues entwined, she moaned low in her throat and wrapped her long legs around his waist.

He tore his mouth from her to ask, "Are you ready for me?"

"Yes," she moaned, her fingers running up and down his back. Her nails raked across his skin, the sweet pain turning him on like nothing else ever had.

With one quick thrust he was inside her, pleasure gripping his body. She was wet and warm, her sex tightening around him.

He groaned and thrust deeper into her, making her cry out in ecstasy. His gaze met hers, and he couldn't look away. Never wanted to.

There was a mix of lust, love, and sadness as her emerald green eyes burned into him. As he rocked into her faster, harder, it was as if they were saying goodbye to each other. Not with words, but with their bodies. With the way she gripped him so tightly, he thought she might never let him go. With each frenzied stroke into her, he was reminding her without words that he loved her more than life itself.

They climaxed together, the pleasure so overwhelming that he collapsed on top of her. When he finally caught his breath, he kissed her damp forehead. "I love you," he told her.

She stared deep into his eyes. "And I love you. Always." Allyson pressed her soft lips to his, a kiss so lingering that it felt like a goodbye.

He had worried that the fear of losing her meant he wouldn't be able to sleep tonight, but he was so exhausted that he closed his eyes and drifted off into dreamless sleep.

Dane awoke with a start, reaching his arm across the bed for his wife. Nothing. Her side of the bed was still warm, but Allyson wasn't sleeping beside him like he expected.

Not to mention their suite was dark.

His eyes darted around the room, searching for her. "Allyson?"

No answer.

She wasn't in their suite. He didn't know how he knew, but he just knew. Dane wasn't the kind of man who panicked, but he was on the verge of turning the place upside down to find her.

Rolling out of bed he grabbed his clothes off the floor, quickly put them on, and started searching the suite for his wife. Every room was empty.

He grabbed his phone, dialing her frantically, but each call instantly went straight to voicemail.

Where was she? Had she left the room to get something downstairs? Had the person who had left that threatening note taken her?

His gut churned. Dane rushed out of their suite and headed downstairs to the front desk.

"Have you seen my wife?" he asked the receptionist. "Allyson Prescott."

"Oh, yes sir, I have," the receptionist answered. "She just headed outside to the rental car."

Rental car? He didn't bother asking the receptionist further questions. Instead he sped out of the lobby and out of the hotel.

It was still dark outside. Probably about three in the morning from the looks of things. A black car was parked right outside, its engine still running.

His wife was sitting in the passenger seat.

Her eyes widened when she saw him. They widened even more as she watched him get into the driver's seat beside her.

"What are you doing?" she demanded.

Teeth gritted he fired back, "What am I doing? What the hell are you doing?"

"Dane, go back inside."

"Not happening," he said. "Not until you tell me where you're going and what you're doing."

She let out a loud sigh. "I'm going to the airport."

"Without me," he muttered.

"That's right," she said with a nod. "I'm going back to New York to take the plea deal."

"The plea deal we both decided was for me," he said. "You made a promise to let me take care of this. I let you look for a way to clear your name. I gave you that chance when we were at Nicholas Handel's place. Now you're just going to break your promise to me?"

"Yes."

"You lied to me," he accused.

"I did," she said. "I knew you wouldn't listen to reason, so I planned to take the plea deal. Lester and I discussed it when you were on the phone with your lawyer. There's a plea deal, and it stands whether you or I show up in New York. As long as one of us shows up, the deal is good. I'm going to take the deal in your place."

"Not any more you're not," he said coldly. "You're going back into the hotel while I head to the airport."

"I'll go away for three years," she said. "It's not that long." She sounded so aloof. So cold and distant. Nothing like herself at all.

"What happened to wanting to clear your name?" he asked.

"After I realized you were going to take the fall for me, I decided saving you was more important than my pride," she said. "You're the one who thought taking a plea deal was a sensible move."

"Yes, if I was the one taking the fall for you," he forced out.

"I can't let you go to jail for something you didn't do."

"But you're innocent, too," he insisted.

She nodded. "I am, but the cops had their sights on me. I brought this problem to our family, so I have to find a solution. This is the best plan."

"I'm not letting you do this." He glared at her.

"That doesn't matter," she said smoothly, in a tone that irritated him. "Lester will be back soon to drive me to the airport. He went to get some cash out of the hotel safe, so I suggest you go back upstairs before he returns."

"Let's just to back to our room to talk this over," he said, hoping to buy more time to get some sense into her before she ruined her life.

"No," she said sharply. "You don't get it, do you? My mother was right about me. I am ruthless and cunning. At least, when I have to be. And, right now, I have to be."

Before he could reply she leaned over, grabbed the car keys from the ignition, and scrambled out of the car.

He reached over to open the passenger door, but it was too late. The *click* of the doors locking let him know that his wife had locked him inside.

"Open the damn door!" he yelled.

She peered in at him, her gaze hard. "That's not going to happen."

"I'll never forgive you for this," he growled.

"As long as you're safe and out of prison, I don't care," she said bluntly.

She turned on her heel and started to walk away from the car, the streetlights overhead illuminating her and the path before her.

Rage surged within him. The thought of her suffering behind bars for years was driving him insane. He swore loudly. His phone was upstairs, inside their suite, so he had no way of trying to call Lester to demand he get some sense into her. If he didn't get out of this car his wife would probably get a head start to take a taxi to the airport and get to New York before him.

Suddenly, a hooded figure appeared out of the darkness beyond the streetlights. Was it Lester?

The figure approached Allyson and raised its hands, wielding a baseball bat. The cherry-red Prescott logo on the baseball bat was unmistakable. Horror made his chest tighten so much he couldn't breathe.

His wife held up her hands defensively, but the figure brought the bat down on her head.

Whatever self-control Dane possessed vanished. He started shouting his wife's name, pounding on the glass of the windshield in a futile effort to save her. The moment the bat connected with her head the second time, Allyson crumpled in a heap on the ground.

The figure leaned over her body, grabbed her bag, and then ran off into the darkness. Dane kept pounding on the glass with his fists so hard he thought he must have broken his hands. He shouted at the top of his lungs, knowing there was no way he could get out of the car to save her.

Chapter 13

She was trapped. Stuck in a nightmare with no way to escape. Darkness swirled all around her. Allyson forced herself to stand. When she tried to run, she tripped and fell hard onto the cold stone floor. The vise around her ankle tightened. She stared down at it, the sight of the shackle around her ankle making her heart sink like a stone. What the hell was going on?

Her eyes snapped open. No. This wasn't right either. The darkness had given way to a white so bright she could hardly see. A tube was protruding from her arm and the whiteness started to spin.

And then she saw blue. A pair of indescribably blue eyes that pulled her out of the abyss.

"Allyson? Can you hear me?" Dane's voice. Her husband's voice.

With her heart pounding, she seized her husband's hand in desperation. "What's happening?"

"You're in the hospital," he said in a low voice. "You're safe now."

A groan escaped her throat. The whiteness began to stop spinning, and after a few moments she saw she was in a private hospital room. Propped up on a bed, hooked up to an IV. "My head," she rasped.

"You have a concussion," he said. "You were wearing a hat, which protected you. If you hadn't..."

Hazy memories flashed in her mind. The darkness. A streetlight overhead. A baseball bat coming down on her. A wave of nausea hit her.

She'd been attacked. Someone had actually beaten her up. Why in the world would someone do that? "Did they find who did this?"

"Not yet." His jaw clenched, and his blue eyes darkened with fury. "Whoever did this better hope to hell the cops find them first. Did you see who it was?"

"No. They were wearing a mask and a hoodie." She shook her head and rubbed her temple. Her head hurt, but not as much as she thought it should. Still, she couldn't shake the dizziness. "I feel woozy," she croaked.

"That's probably the drugs." He sat down in the chair beside her, but didn't let go of her hand. "You've been here since last night. For a second I thought I'd lost you. I thought that bastard was going to kill you." His voice was thick with emotion. Sadness. And something else. Rage.

Her heart squeezed in terror at the thought of what her husband might do to find out who had done this to her. "I'm still here. I don't they were trying to kill me."

"I doubt it was just a robbery," he said, casting her a flinty stare.

"What do you mean?" she asked.

"They took your bag," he said, "but it couldn't have been a routine mugging. It looked too...efficient to be something that desperate and random."

"My bag..." Her eyelids fluttered closed momentarily as she tried to remember. "The will. Nicholas Handel's will was in my bag."

He swore under his breath. "Dammit! Your attacker must've known."

"How?" she demanded, and then winced, lowing her voice. "Nobody knew I had the will in there. Not even you."

"No, but Nicholas must have figured out that the will went missing," he pointed out.

Allyson forced herself to remember the attack. Her stomach churned at the memory. She had been walking away from the car, trying to flee back to New York. And then, out of nowhere, a hooded figure had appeared and beaten her down with a baseball bat.

She wracked her brain, trying to remember what the attacker looked like, but the mask and hoodie had hidden everything. And it had been so dark. She didn't even know what color her attacker's eyes were. "You don't think Nicholas was the one who attacked me, do you?" she asked in horror.

"Who else could it have been?" His hold on her hand tightened. "I'll kill him. I'll kill him for what he did to you—"

"We don't know that it was him," she insisted.

"If it wasn't him, it was someone he sent," Dane said coldly.

"Look, Nicky can be a jerk, but you don't actually think he'd beat me with a bat, do you?"

"It's exactly what I think," her husband muttered. "It was a Prescott bat, for one thing."

"Plenty of people have Prescott baseball bats," she said.

"Including Nicholas Handel," he said.

She shivered at his tone. Dane wasn't going to let this go. Her husband might have good breeding and have been born into a privileged family, but he was ruthless when it came to protecting her. It didn't matter if Nicholas Handel had actually attacked her. Dane believed he had, and that meant Nicholas had a target on his back.

"What do we do now?" she asked.

"I called your parents," he said. "They're worried. I had to beg them not to get on a flight out to London."

"Thank you." She was grateful that her husband knew her well enough to understand that, while her family deserved to know that she had been hurt, she didn't want to face them right now. Didn't want to see them after the argument she'd had with her mother. They probably all believed she was a thief, and she was in no state to defend herself. "How long do I have to stay in the hospital?"

"Not much longer," he replied. "The doctor said that, at most, you'll spend another night here. If thinks you look good you might even be out of here later today."

"Thank goodness," she said, breathing a sigh of relief. After her attacker had raised the baseball bat to strike, she had momentarily believed he was going to do far worse damage. Maybe even kill her. She shuddered at the thought. Whoever had attacked her must have been desperate to get the will back.

"After that I'll be heading back to New York to take the plea deal," he said.

"What?" She sat up straighter. Her head throbbed with pain, but she ignored it. "No. I left so that you wouldn't have to face this."

"You really think you're in a fit state to hand yourself over to the court?" His eyes narrowed. "Allyson, you could have been killed. There's no way you can survive three minutes in jail, much less three years."

"I survived a night in lockup—"

"While dressed in an evening gown—"

"What? You think I'm too spoiled to go to prison?" she snapped.

He sighed heavily. "I think that, as my wife, you're not going to prison. No wife of mine is going to jail. This is not what I married you for."

Tears stung her eyes. "Please don't do this."

"Allyson, I thought that son of a bitch had killed you," he forced out. "I thought you were dead. That's why I tried to break the damn windows in the car to get to you."

It was then that she noticed the bandages around his knuckles. She gasped. "You're hurt."

"I tried to punch through the glass like a damn fool," he confessed. "Thank God Lester came back outside as quickly as he did. He's the one who called the ambulance while I watched over you."

She tried to imagine what it would like to watch someone attack Dane so badly she thought that he might die. Just imagining it felt like a crushing weight on her chest. There was no way she could stand to see something that unspeakable.

No wonder he was so adamant about protecting her now. In her rush to protect him from prison she had gotten hurt, and caused him so much more suffering than she had ever planned or imagined. Forcing him to watch her go away to prison was one thing. But Dane thinking she was dying must have been ten-thousand times worse.

Dane raised her hand to his lips, the kiss heating her all over. "I'm doing this. No man could let the woman he loves suffer like this. I'm your husband. It's my job to protect you. Let me do my job."

She brushed her tears away. "Why are you so old-fashioned?"

"Because I come from an old family," he said. "No more arguments. All I ask is that you wait for me."

"Of course, I'll wait for you. I love you."

He leaned over to plant a kiss on her forehead. She shut her eyes, the sensation of his lips on her skin making her heart ache with a longing she didn't even know was possible. How was it possible for her to miss her husband when he was still right here with her?

Three years without him. It was a better deal than thirty years apart, but she knew that the next three years would be the longest of her life. She choked back a sob, trying to be strong. It was probably her injury that had made her relent to his demands. Guilt was eating her alive. Dane was going to pay for something he didn't do, on her behalf. She had no idea how she was going to live with herself.

A nurse appeared. "You have some visitors. Are you feeling strong enough?"

Allyson exchanged a glance with Dane. "Visitors?"

"My dad," he replied. "He's been worried sick about you."

"Oh, poor guy—let him in," Allyson said.

The nurse nodded and stepped back out. Moments later, Dane's father and his assistant, Fran, walked into the room.

Alfred's face was pale with worry. "You're all right."

Allyson nodded. "Yes. I feel a bit dizzy, but I'm glad to be okay."

"Are you doing well enough to speak to Lester?" Alfred asked. "He wanted to talk to you about the plea deal. He isn't sure if Dane is still going to go in your place."

"Let me talk to Lester," Dane said.

"That's probably for the best. We can let Allyson get some rest while we tie up loose ends with Lester." Alfred turned to Fran. "Can you stay with Mrs. Prescott until we come back?"

"Of course, sir," Fran replied.

With that, Dane and his father headed out of the room. Allyson felt a twinge of regret as she watched them leave together. Dane and his father were very close. And now, after Alfred's heart attack, he had to deal with his only son going to prison for three years.

Despair tore at her. She was on the verge of tears again, but she refused to cry in front of Francesca Barnes. Not after all the awful things Fran had said about her to Katherine that day in the bathroom at Prescott Global.

She eyed Fran warily as the young assistant sat down beside her.

Fran bit her lip. "Look...I know that we aren't exactly friends—"

"No, we're not," Allyson said sourly, in too much pain to bother being civil. "Not after you disparaged me to Katherine Handel in the bathroom."

Fran's eyes went wide. Her hand flew to her mouth, shame etched on her lovely heart-shaped face. "Oh, crap. You heard that."

"I did," Allyson replied through clenched teeth. "You called me common, if I remember correctly."

"Now I understand why you don't like me anymore," she said miserably. "Allyson...I mean, Mrs. Prescott...I was an idiot. I was wrong to talk about you like that. Especially to a woman like Katherine Handel."

The venom in Fran's voice when she mentioned Katherine was unmistakable.

"What do you know about Katherine?" Allyson asked, hoping that maybe Fran might know something about the Handels that could save Dane from prison.

"I know that she's a liar," Fran spat out. "I was her confidante. Told her every piece of gossip I heard about you and Mr. Prescott's relationship. In exchange she promised to get me a good job, but after she ran off back to England she totally screwed me over. There had never even been a job. She just lied to get me to do what she wanted."

"That sounds like Katherine," Allyson said. "I just want to know if you've heard anything in relation to the embezzlement. I know it sounds crazy, but Dane suspects the Handels set me up. We need to get the real culprit."

"I don't know." Fran bit her lip, her eyes darting around the room. "The Handels can be so vindictive. My family is going through financial trouble because my brother's ex-wife took everything from us, and I don't want to make the Handels angry. They're so powerful."

Allyson sighed. There was a chance that Fran had heard something, but pushing her too hard for information might backfire. Instead, she made a mental note to gently pry for more information later. "I understand, believe me. Going against them can be dangerous, especially if you're trying to keep your head down and help your family."

Fran nodded. "Again, I'm so sorry about those awful things I said about you."

"Forget about it," Allyson said. "I've got way bigger problems than office gossip."

Dane reappeared in the room, catching Allyson's attention. He did not look happy. At all.

Her stomach churned. The nausea was coming back. "What is it?"

"It's not good," he replied. "Lester got a call from New York from the prosecutor. The plea deal is off the table."

Chapter 14

She gasped. "How can the plea deal be off the table?"

The look on her face made him clench his fists in rage. His plans to save his wife were crumbling. All because a judge back in New York thought Allyson was a liar. "The judge who granted you bail found out about the attack."

Her face was pale. She had never looked so fragile than she did in this moment. In a hospital bed, hooked up to an IV. All because some coward had assaulted her. "So, what does this mean?" She was putting on a brave face, but he saw fear flicker in her eyes.

Dane quickly crossed the room and sat down on the hospital bed. Being near her might comfort her. "The prosecutor told the judge about the attack after Lester called him with the news. The judge thinks we faked the attack to get out of coming back to New York and facing jail time."

"What? I would never do something like that," she cried.

"I know. But that's not how the judge sees it. So, the prosecutor has taken the plea deal off the table. For both of us," he said. "He wants you back in New York City as soon as possible."

"When's the trial, then?" she asked. "Maybe I'll at least still have time to clear my name."

Agony pierced his insides. "The trial date hasn't been set, but we're running out of time."

"So, this is real. I'll actually have to face a jury?" she whispered.

He nodded. "Yes."

Her face blanched. "I'll have to go through the whole process. Jury selection. All of it."

"Lester says getting character witnesses will be crucial," he replied.

"So, basically, I have to trust other people to save me," she said.

He reached for her small hand and squeezed it. "We're going to fight this. Maybe we won't have to go to trial. If we fight hard enough, we can get the plea deal back so that I can go in your place."

"Oh, Dane." Tears streamed down her face. "I'm scared."

He knew that Allyson had originally rejected the idea of taking a guilty plea so that she could clear her name, but now that she was facing a trial she must be terrified. No way was he going to let his wife suffer this. "We're going to fight this. I'm not letting anything bad happen to you."

Lester stepped into the room, shoving his phone into his jacket pocket. "I just got off the phone with the judge. He still insists that you come back to New York, but I've managed to buy you four days."

The fact that Lester had gotten the judge to let his wife take a few days to get back to the States was a minor miracle, but Dane still felt his blood begin to boil. "Why is the judge doing this? Look at the state of her. It's obvious someone attacked her. We can prove it happened."

"You can't prove that you didn't set it up to get out of having to return to face jail time," Lester replied grimly. "Look, the police are outside waiting for a statement. I can't act as your lawyer, Mr. Prescott, so my advice is to let Mrs. Prescott give the statement while I'm here with her."

Dane nodded and brought his wife's hand to his lips. He kissed it lovingly. "I'll be right outside if you need me."

"Okay," she said softly.

He and Fran headed out of the hospital room while two police officers headed inside to interview Allyson.

When the interview was over, the police officers handed out their contact information and left. After that, Allyson was discharged from the hospital and they all headed back to the hotel.

"I think we should have a quick meeting to discuss strategy going forward," Allyson said in the elevator up to their suite.

Dane frowned. "You need to rest."

She bit her lip. "I know, but now I have to deal with a trial. Plus, I don't think I can get much rest with my attacker still out there. It's all become..."

"A bit of a shit-show?"

She scoffed and touched her forehead. "You could say that. Or worse."

Taking her hand in his, Dane pressed a kiss against her cheek. "We can always change hotels. And I have contacts with a private security firm. We can have them send over some bodyguards as quickly as possible."

His wife leaned against him, her entire body seeming to droop under the weight of so much stress. He wrapped his arms around her tightly, trying to steady her.

"I don't really want someone shadowing me," she said, her voice strained. "Maybe just have extra security outside the hotel."

"I can arrange that," he assured her.

When the elevator stopped on their floor Fran and his father headed to their own rooms while Dane, Allyson, and Lester walked to their luxury suite for a meeting.

Dane helped Allyson to the sofa in the sitting area, reluctant to even leave her side for a moment. Pushing aside his concern, he focused on what he could do to help her. If she couldn't get rest, she could at least eat to get her strength up. After he ordering room service, he sat beside Allyson and wrapped his arm around her shoulders.

"We have to figure out where our focus needs to be," Lester said from his seat on the opposite sofa.

"What do you mean?" Dane asked.

"Are we going to focus on getting the charges dropped entirely, or are we going to focus on winning a trial?" Lester said.

"Well, what's your advice?" Dane asked. Lester was a damn good lawyer, and Dane knew it would be wise to listen to him.

"I'm not going to lie to you. The prosecution is out for blood," Lester said. "They want someone to pay for a white-collar crime like this since they're often accused of going soft on the rich. But a trial is costly and attracts media attention they might not like."

"So, should we try to get the charges dropped?" Allyson asked.

Lester scratched his chin thoughtfully. "The prosecution has circumstantial evidence, but nothing concrete. At least, not yet. Which means there's still a chance we can get the charges dropped completely. We'll have less time to gather more of our own evidence than if we focused our efforts on a trial, but we still have a chance to make this whole thing go away."

"What kind of evidence do we need?" she asked.

"Anything that could cast doubt on you being the embezzler," Lester responded. "Our best bet is to point the authorities to someone else."

"So...we have to figure out who did this." Allyson sighed. "The person who attacked me snatched my handbag out of my hands. Nicholas Handel's will was inside it."

Lester grimaced. "It wasn't exactly found under legal circumstances, but at least it was a lead. Things seem to be pointing in the direction of Nicholas Handel or his wife."

Never had he wanted to hurt someone more than he wanted to hurt Nicholas Handel. Nicholas had to be responsible for the attack. He had to. Dane could feel it in his bones. "If Nicholas did this, I'll make him pay. Do you remember anything about the guy who hit you?"

She shook her head. The sad expression on her face knifed through him. Allyson was shaking like a leaf. The attack must have been traumatic for her. Just watching her get hit with a baseball bat like that almost destroyed him. He couldn't begin to understand what it was like to go through it.

Desperate to soothe her, he rubbed her shoulder gently.

"It was so dark I didn't get a good look at their face. I don't even know what color his eyes were." She began to wring her hands, anxiety etched on her face. "He was thin, slightly taller than me. That's all I know."

"The cops will be looking over the CCTV footage of the attack," Lester said. "They've assured me that they'll get in touch if they discover anything."

"It feels like we've hit a dead end," Allyson said.

Dane shook his head. "I'm not giving up. We're going to get some hard evidence against Nicholas. I'm not letting the bastard get away with hurting you like this. It's looking like Nicholas Handel either attacked you himself or sent someone to do it."

Lester frowned. "Nicholas Handel isn't the type to get his hands dirty. If he's involved, he more than likely sent someone to hurt Mrs. Prescott."

"But how could he have known that I had taken the will?" Allyson asked. "Dane made sure to keep him from walking into the study and finding me."

"Maybe he saw you head in that direction and put two and two together," Dane suggested.

She sighed. "I guess that's possible. I just don't see how he could have figured out that I had the will in that handbag. It wasn't the same bag I had at the party. Nobody knew it was in there but me."

That must have shaken her, the fact that someone had figured out what she had and where she had put it. Almost like Nicholas had spies watching them. Or was watching them himself. It sounded crazy, but the entire business with the embezzlement was beyond anything he'd ever had to deal with. His own father had worried about what the embezzler might do to keep his secret. For all they knew, the attacker wouldn't stop at one assault on Allyson. The next time might be something much worse. Something permanent.

White-hot rage gripped him. And underneath it, an emotion he rarely felt. Fear. Fear for his wife's safety. "I'm not going to let you stay in this hotel another night," Dane said suddenly.

"You think we should leave?" she asked.

He nodded. "If the attacker knew that much, there's no telling what else he might figure out. We've got to get out of here."

Lester glanced at Allyson. "Your husband is probably right. Find a place to stay for the next few days while we figure this out."

"We can stay at my cousin's apartment," Dane said. "Ordinarily I wouldn't ask since he isn't in London, but desperate times..."

Allyson nodded. "Okay. Since you think it would help."

It wasn't like her to just give in and accept his demands. Usually Allyson put up one hell of a fight. Or, maybe she was doing what she had done last night. Agreed to something only to have her own plans. Promise she'd go along with what he wanted, only to ruthlessly do what she thought she had to do.

His guts twisting he captured her chin in his hand, forcing her to look at him. "I mean it, Allyson. We're leaving the hotel. Don't even think of getting any ideas. You're not running this time. You won't get rid of me that easily if you try a stunt like that again."

She lowered her eyes, those dark eyelashes brushing against her flushed cheeks. "Not in front of Lester."

"I don't give a damn if Lester sees," he bit out harshly. "You are my wife. The only thing in this world I care about more than myself. I almost lost you. Never do something like that to me ever again."

If she bristled at his words, she didn't show it. All she did was nod. She looked so fragile and vulnerable that he couldn't help but wrap his arms around her and pull her close.

Gripping him tightly, her shoulders started to heave. "I thought he was going to kill me. And after he hit me, I thought he was going to find a way to hurt you, Dane. I was so scared." A sob escaped her throat, the sound like a dagger in his heart.

He held her. Kissed her hair. "We'll get him. I swear we'll find him and make him pay for this."

She was crying now. He could feel her tears on his shirt.

The sound of Lester's cell phone ringing made him glance over at the lawyer. As Lester took the call, Dane gently rocked his wife back and forth. Whispered into her ear that he loved her.

"It's my fault," she said. "If I hadn't locked you in the car...if I hadn't gotten out of the car like a stubborn idiot—"

"It's not your fault," he said gently. "Nobody has the right to hurt you. Nobody. It's not your fault, Allyson. We're going to catch the bastard. I promise you."

She pressed her mouth to his and he tasted the salty tears on her lips. Tasted her anguish. Her terror.

A low cough from Lester made her pull away suddenly.

"We have some bad news folks." Lester put his phone back into his jacket pocket. "That was the judge's office calling."

"What is it?" Allyson asked, her voice shaky.

Then Lester said the words that ripped Dane's heart apart: "The judge is revoking your bail. He wants you to turn yourself in and go back to jail until the trial."

Chapter 15

Allyson's blood ran cold. Or maybe it stopped moving completely. The fear that had been building within her since her arrest threatened to overwhelm her. It felt like the floor beneath her had given way and she was falling into the dark abyss.

"Back to jail?" Her voice wavered as tears threatened to fall again.

Dane cursed loudly. "Crane, get the judge back on the phone. We're not putting up with his. The bail has been paid. My wife isn't spending another second in jail, do you hear me?" An inferno blazed dangerously in his blue eyes. "She'll stay here. Never go back to America."

Lester shook his head vigorously. "I wouldn't advise that. And arguing with the judge will only make things worse for Mrs. Prescott. He already believes the attack was faked and, considering your reputation for...phony stories, he isn't inclined to listen."

She groaned inwardly. The world was never going to let go of the fact that she and Dane had faked their marriage at the start of their relationship. That was why it was so easy for everyone to believe the worst about her. "So, I'm supposed to just turn myself over to the police?" she asked. Stomach knotting up she swallowed hard, trying to fight the mounting terror.

"We still have four days to get back to New York," Lester said. "But, yes...if you don't turn yourself over for arrest within that time, you'll be a fugitive." He paused, sympathy flashing in his eyes. "I'm sorry, Mrs. Prescott."

Memories of her night in jail made her shudder. Those imposing bars haunted her dreams. The hours she spent in jail had inched by so slowly that one night had been a lifetime. Panic made her pulse race. "So, are we just going to give up on getting the charges dropped?"

"No," her husband said firmly. "We don't have a lot of time now, but I'm going to turn this city upside down if I have to. I'm not letting them put you away."

His words both comforted her and terrified her. She knew he would do anything to keep her safe. There was nothing her husband wouldn't do to keep her out of jail. He had almost broken his hands last night, trying to break the windshield of the car in an insane effort to get to her. Despite the comfort she felt, she also knew that her husband would risk anything. If he was willing to risk prison time and getting injured, he was liable to do something even crazier.

"Now that Nicholas Handel's will has been taken, we don't have many leads," Lester pointed out.

Lost in thought, Allyson chewed her bottom lip. "Francesca seemed to know something. Earlier today, in the hospital, she was reluctant to tell me something about the Handels. Not to mention, I still have serious suspicions about Rebecca Greene since she works in the women's division at the London office."

"My money is on Nicholas Handel," Dane growled. "It has to be. There's no way he doesn't know about his wife's trust."

"He wouldn't have given us access to such sensitive files if he was the culprit," Lester reminded them.

"Maybe Nicholas didn't know at the start of all this, but if he discovered what his wife was up to he might have decided to protect her," Dane said.

Allyson inhaled sharply. "Oh crap. You have a point." Nicholas couldn't have known about his heir's secret trust when he gave them all those files, but there was a chance he had discovered the truth about his wife's stealing and was doing whatever it took to keep the secret. Even if that meant going after her with a baseball bat.

"We have to figure out who Nicholas Handel's heir is if we want to figure this out," Lester said. "Which is easier said than done, but we can start with Rebecca like you suggested, Mrs. Prescott."

Dane crossed his arms. "First things first. We have to get Allyson safely out of the hotel."

"We don't have much time," she said, trying to keep the frantic edge out of her tone.

Her husband got to his feet. "That's why, after I make arrangements with my cousin, we'll talk to Fran in the car and look into Rebecca Greene."

After Dane's cousin agreed to let them stay at his place Allyson texted Francesca, asking her to meet them downstairs in the lobby.

Ten minutes later, Allyson and Dane had packed up their belongings and made their way downstairs with Lester. While Dane went to the front desk to deal with checking out, Allyson headed outside with Fran and Lester.

Suddenly, Nicholas Handel and Rebecca Green stepped out of a luxury car parked at the front entrance. Nicholas took off his coat and draped it around Rebecca's shoulders.

Allyson watched them suspiciously as they headed over to her. Outwardly, Rebecca Greene had a very nerd-chic vibe about her. The total opposite of what a man like Nicholas seemed to be interested in. But he also had a thing for intelligent women, and Rebecca had a very intellectual air with her hair tied up in a prim bun and her glasses perched on her nose.

Everyone quickly exchanged greetings.

"What are you doing here?" Allyson blurted out.

Nicholas pulled her into a tight hug. "We heard what happened, and when we realized you had been discharged from hospital we came down here to see you. Thank goodness you're okay, Allyson."

She squirmed out of his embrace, memories of last night's attack setting her on edge in his presence. Allyson didn't know if Nicholas had attacked her, but he was the last person she wanted to see right now. "I'm fine," she said bluntly. "You don't have to check up on me."

"Of course, we do," Nicholas insisted. "I know we've had our differences, but after an incident like this we have to stick together."

Before she could open her mouth to retort, Dane shot out in front of her. More like his fist, which got into Nicky's face, and punched him in the nose.

"STAY THE HELL AWAY from my wife!" Pain shot through his hand. Dane had nearly broken his hands trying to save Allyson last night, but he didn't care if he broke his hand for real this time.

Blood spurted out of Nicholas' nose as he howled in agony. "What the bloody hell is wrong with you?"

Dane lunged at Nicholas again, but a pair of strong hands dragged him back. It was Lester. Pulling him back into the hotel lobby. Rage making it impossible to think clearly, Dane shoved Lester away.

"You stay here," Lester hissed. "I'm going to take care of this."

"Why?" Dane demanded. "That bastard attacked my wife—"

"I'm going back out there to talk to Nicholas and avoid a damn lawsuit," Lester cut him off harshly. "Heaven help us if Handel goes to the cops and presses charges." The lawyer turned on his heel and headed back outside.

Allyson stepped back into the lobby, Rebecca following.

"Why did you do that?" Allyson asked. She knew why, but she asked anyway.

"He attacked you," he snarled. "Nobody hurts you and gets away with it."

Seeing Nicholas show up at the hotel like he'd done nothing wrong had sent Dane into a blind rage. He didn't care if it was reckless. If he ever saw Nicholas Handel's face again he would tear him apart.

"You've probably broken his nose," she said.

The guests in the lobby turned to stare at them, but he ignored their glances. Right now, the only thing that mattered was keeping his wife safe from the Handels. "If he tries to come near you again, a broken nose is going to be the least of his worries," Dane muttered.

"I did warn him not to come," Rebecca Greene murmured.

Dane frowned as he turned to her. "Warn him?"

Rebecca shifted uncomfortably, then adjusted her glasses. "I told Mr. Handel that, given your history, you might suspect him. The hostility between the Handels and the Prescotts isn't exactly a secret."

He narrowed his eyes at her. "You're that close to him?"

"Well, I am one of Prescott Global's most senior executives here in London," Rebecca replied.

"That's the only reason you're close to him?" Allyson asked. "You're not part of the family or anything like that?"

Rebecca tilted her head. "I don't follow."

"Are you married to Nicholas Handel?" Dane asked through clenched teeth.

Rebecca's eyes widened in surprise. "Good heavens! You think..." She squared her shoulders. "I'm married, but not to Mr. Handel. Mr. Handel isn't even married."

"That's what you think," he muttered, watching her closely. Despite her denial, he still didn't trust Rebecca or anyone connected to Nicholas.

"So, you're married, but not to Nicholas," Allyson said. "Why wasn't your husband at the party at Nicholas' apartment? Why aren't you wearing a ring?"

"Who says I'm not?" Rebecca asked. In exasperation she reached under the collar of her blouse and pulled out a necklace with a ring hanging from it. Dane exchanged a knowing glance with his wife, recognition in Allyson's eyes. Rebecca wore her ring the same way Allyson had when they were first engaged.

"And if you must know," Rebecca continued, "my husband is a surgeon doing charity work overseas. That's why he wasn't at the work party." With a roll of her eyes she pulled a wallet from her handbag and handed it over to Allyson. "There are photos of Neville, and some of his business cards. Why don't you have a look?"

Allyson bit her lip. "I don't know—"

"I'll look." Dane took the wallet from Allyson and started to inspect the contents. He wasn't a fool. Rebecca might just be pretending to be outraged, so he made sure to look through her wallet. It wasn't exactly the best manners, but if Allyson could be saved by him being a jerk then he was willing to take the risk.

Satisfied that she was telling the truth, he handed Rebecca her wallet. "Your story seems to check out," he said tightly.

"Of course, it does," Rebecca said sharply. "But one person's story absolutely does not check out."

He raised an eyebrow, suddenly curious. "Who?"

Rebecca leaned forward. "Nicholas," she replied, lowering her voice. "He's been acting strangely since the party. Ordinarily I wouldn't say anything to disparage my boss, but after I heard that you had been viciously attacked, Mrs. Prescott, I started to wonder if I should tell you what I know."

"What do you know, Rebecca?" his wife asked softly.

Rebecca looked around to make sure they weren't being overheard. Then she leaned in closer. "I overheard Mr. Handel on the telephone last night as the party was ending, after you had all left. He was having a terrible row with someone. He kept going on and on about not having any money left to give. It sounded like someone was blackmailing him. Like the person on the other end of the call knew he had done something terrible, and wanted to be bought off with money."

"The embezzlement," Allyson breathed. "Someone knows he's done something terrible, or is covering for someone. The blackmailer is probably using it against him."

"That's what it sounded like," Rebecca said with a nod. "And very soon after that call you were attacked."

"Could you testify to something like this?" Dane asked.

Rebecca's face paled. "No. Please. Don't make me get involved with the police. It could ruin me. My husband and I need me to keep this job. His salary isn't enough for us to survive on."

He held up his hands, trying to reassure her. "My wife could be getting framed for something she didn't do. She could end up going to prison for decades because of this. I'm begging you, Rebecca."

"I do have proof," Rebecca said. "I recorded what I heard. It sounded so strange that I recorded it on my phone."

"Can we hear it?" Allyson bit her lip.

"That's just it," Rebecca murmured. "I saved the recording on my mobile phone. It's a company phone, and I was so nervous about the recording that I left my mobile at home."

"So, we can still listen to it?" Allyson asked. "We can go get it now."

Suddenly, Lester appeared, concern etched on his face. "Folks, we have to get out of London. Now."

"Why?" Allyson asked.

"I couldn't talk Nicholas out of letting you off the hook for punching him." Lester glared at Dane. "It's probably best that we get you both on the jet and back to New York pronto."

"We might have a lead," Allyson said.

"Rebecca might have something that could clear Allyson's name," Dane said. At this point, things were getting desperate. They needed to get their hands on whatever evidence they could to save his wife from prison.

"Look, if you don't want to face another set of criminal charges, you have to get back to the States," Lester said. "If we get mixed up with the cops coming after you, Mr. Prescott, that takes time away from Mrs. Prescott's own case. And we can't afford to waste time with the judge's order hanging over us."

Dane swore. "Let them arrest me. Focus on Allyson."

"Isn't your father still in London?" Rebecca asked. "I could play the recording for him. Would his testimony be enough?"

Allyson glanced at Lester, and quickly filled him on what Rebecca had told them about the recording.

"If your father hears the recording and transcribes what he hears, that might be enough to buy us some time," Lester said. "Make the grounds shaky and maybe get the prosecution to rethink the charges. But we have to get on a plane as soon as possible. Getting arrested for punching a member of your own staff isn't exactly going to endear you to the press or the authorities, Mr. Prescott."

With a heavy sigh, Dane nodded. "Fine. We'll head back to New York. But I want my father to hear this recording as soon as he can."

"I'll arrange it," Lester said.

After saying their rushed goodbyes to Rebecca, they got into the rental car and raced towards the airport. Dane took his wife's hand in his. Her face was pale, and she looked exhausted. Now, the only thing keeping her from jail was the word of a woman they barely knew.

And Dane still wasn't sure if he trusted Rebecca Greene.

Chapter 16

When they touched down at JFK, Allyson expected to find an army of police in the terminal waiting for her. Along with the news and reporters. Luckily, none of the uniformed officers in the airport were there to arrest her, but that didn't stop the flood of paranoia.

After they landed they took a taxi home to their apartment, with Lester insisting they all meet to go over what to do next.

Lester whipped out his phone to read his messages. "Your father will be in New York within the next four hours. He listened to the recording, and it sounds like we have some compelling evidence."

She breathed a sigh of relief and flopped down on the sofa in the living room. Maybe this nightmare would be over soon. Then she and Dane could get back to living their lives. Finally move in to their dream house.

It felt like the day Dane had bought the house was years and years ago. She had been so happy. So ready to start a new chapter of their lives together.

Dane tossed off his jacket and sat down beside her. "So, what now?"

Lester glanced at his watch. "It's after 8 o'clock, so it's too late to call the judge or the prosecutor tonight. I'll contact them first thing in the morning to set up a preliminary hearing. If your father's testimony is good enough, we might be able to get the charges dropped as early as tomorrow afternoon. I hope we can just end this in the morning."

"What about Nicholas going to the police?" she asked. "He didn't seem too happy about my husband punching him in the face."

Dane shot her a look. "I'm only sorry that I got only one punch in."

"Dane!"

"What? It's obvious he framed you. Which means he attacked you or sent someone to beat you up. A punch in the face is him getting off light," her husband muttered. "When we get the charges against you dropped, I'm going to destroy Nicholas for attacking you."

"The London police will be looking over everything having to do with Mrs. Prescott's attack," Lester said. "Let them deal with that while we keep our focus on getting Mrs. Prescott free."

"Thank you, Lester, for being the voice of reason once again," she said pointedly.

Dane scoffed, but didn't say anything.

They spent the next half-hour going over strategy for the potential hearing until Lester finally said his goodbyes and left.

"Look, I'm sorry for putting you in this position after going after Nicholas," Dane said. Suddenly, he reached down to hook his arm up around her knees and draped her legs over his lap. Her head was up against the armrest of the sofa, and it felt so good to lie back and relax like this. He slipped her shoes off and expertly started massaging her aching feet.

A moan escaped her lips. His hands on her was indescribable. Wonderful. "If you keep touching me like that, I think I can find it in me to forgive you for punching Nicholas in the face," she said breathlessly.

Dane laughed, working his strong hands, releasing the tension in her legs and feet. "I'll do whatever it takes to get back in your good graces."

"You really do spoil me, you know?"

"A beautiful woman like you should always be spoiled." He flashed her that dazzling smile of his, and her heart just about melted. "Not to mention you've had a trying twenty-four hours. I'm going to make sure you get all the rest you can."

"This might all be over soon," she said. Nicholas might try to go after them for getting punched, but after facing a potential thirty years in prison she could handle whatever Nicholas threw at them.

She watched him as he kept his hands on her legs and feet, rubbing firmly, massaging all the pressure out of her muscles.

This ordeal had been so terrifying. And it would have been so much worse without Dane. Life without her husband seemed impossible. He was everything to her. Love made her heart swell so much it nearly ached. Just the thought of the charges being dropped made her feel lighter. More at ease than she had been in days. "I could kiss you," she said.

He arched an eyebrow. "Why don't you?"

"I don't think I have the strength to get up and reward you with a kiss," she murmured. "But Dane, you hurt your hands. You must be in pain."

"It does hurt a little," he admitted with a wince. "But that's nothing compared to what I felt when I was stuck in the car and couldn't get to you. That pain will never heal."

She had put him through something horrible. Allyson didn't regret trying to go to jail to keep him free and safe. But she did regret putting him through an ordeal like that. "I'm sorry for putting you through that. I do love you, you know."

"I know." There was a glint in his eye. As if at any moment he might do more than just massage her. His hands wandered away from her legs, up her skirt, to caress her thighs.

Desire heated her skin. Made the place between her thighs throb with need.

"If you're too tired, I can stop," he said, his voice a low rumble. "But you won't have to do anything other than lie back."

Her lips twisted into a coy smile. "Well, in that case, I'm not that tired."

She should have been exhausted from the flight, but something about the attack had left her reeling. Left her vulnerable and raw. There had been a moment before she blacked out when she really thought she was going to be killed. Leave Dane behind. Or worse, be killed and then have her attacker go after Dane.

Her entire body ached to have him touch her. She needed to share her body with him to feel whole again. To feel alive.

Dane's hands trailed up her thighs until they stopped the waistband of her panties. Face heating, she lifted her skirt and propped up her legs, the anticipation of what he was going to do to her making her heart pound. He tugged at her panties and she lifted her hips, helping him as he peeled off the lacy fabric.

He stared down at her sex, and the lust in his eyes made her wet. Turned her on like nothing ever had. They had been married all these months, been through hell, and yet he still looked at her with hunger burning in his eyes.

As he pressed his mouth against her inner thigh, she shivered. Delight coursed through her. With his lips still against her skin, she felt his mouth curve up into a wolfish smile.

"You're in for it now," he said.

She laughed. "Am I about to be punished?"

"Oh, I'm going to enjoy tormenting you," he growled against her skin. He kissed his way up her thigh, and she quivered beneath his perfect mouth.

When he finally kissed the place between her legs she let out a muffled cry. Pleasure, so intense it almost unraveled her, shot through her core. Just one kiss was enough to almost undo her. His tongue swirled into her wetness. She moaned, squirming beneath him as he gripped her thighs.

Arching her back she pressed against his mouth, desperate for more friction. More contact. He stroked her with his tongue, the rhythm achingly, tortuously, exquisitely slow.

Her body was suddenly molten. Weightless as pleasure radiated through her. "*Yes*." She dug her nails into the sofa, the ecstasy he was giving her already making her lose control.

His tongue swirled into her furiously now, hungrily, like he was enjoying this as much as she was. She whimpered, already on the edge of ecstasy. His hot mouth tormented her. Gave her the sweetest torture of her life.

When she climaxed her body was trembling, the force of her orgasm overwhelming her.

Her husband pulled his mouth away from her and grinned devilishly. Then, he planted hot kisses up and down her thighs. Finally, when she caught her breath, she gave him a small smile.

"You're the most talented man I have ever met," she said.

That made him laugh, and he pulled away to look at her. "You are so beautiful." His hand lazily caressed her inner thigh. "So perfect." The heat in his gaze suddenly gave way to tenderness. "I love you."

She knew that, with the danger that lay in front of them, it was dangerous to hope. But she did just that. Hoped. Because, in this moment, she didn't know how she could possibly survive years without the man she loved.

HE HELD ALLYSON'S HAND as they walked into the courtroom, muscling his way through the throng of reporters. It took everything in him to resist the urge to start shoving journalists away from Allyson. Right now, his wife couldn't afford any more negative press.

The media hadn't gotten wind of his fight with Nicholas, so he wasn't about to give them something to run with now.

Lester walked ahead of them, towards the front.

Allyson turned to press a quick kiss to his lips. "Thank you for coming with me."

Pulling her into his arms, Dane said into her ear, "Trust Lester. He knows what he's doing. I'll be right here. I won't leave you."

He should have been at work, but he wasn't going to let Allyson suffer this hearing alone.

"I love you." She kissed him again, then slipped away from him and headed to sit with Lester at her place before the judge's bench.

He sat down in the back and waited for the hearing to begin.

When the judge entered the courtroom, Dane recognized him. Tyrone Caldwell was a stern man in his early sixties, who ran in the same circles as his parents. Judge Caldwell wasn't exactly a family friend, but Dane remembered him from a golf outing or two in the past. Caldwell wasn't the type for backslapping, and didn't put up with bull. Which was probably why he had been so quick to mercilessly revoke Allyson's bail.

Proceedings began with Lester asking to have the charges against Allyson dropped. Then witnesses were called up to testify, starting with Dane's father. His father handled the questions well, giving an account of the recording he had heard of Nicholas. When the prosecution had the chance to pepper his father with questions he held his own, never cowering.

The last witness called was Francesca Barnes, his father's assistant. Fran had been the one to transcribe the recording of Nicholas, and she could back up his father's account with testimony of her own. Her account was crucial if they wanted to make suspicion of Nicholas credible.

Lester approached her, holding a piece of paper in his hand. "Ms. Barnes, I'd just like to establish that you transcribed this while you were in London. You wrote this transcription while listening to a recording of Mr. Nicholas Handel discussing his financial troubles. Is that correct?"

"No comment," Fran replied.

A low murmur filled the courtroom.

Dane leaned forward in his seat.

Judge Caldwell turned his stern gaze on Fran. "Ms. Barnes, this might not be a trial, but at this hearing you do have to answer. And you have to answer truthfully."

"I did answer truthfully," Fran said. "I cannot comment. I can't very well testify against my own husband, can I?"

"Husband?" Lester approached her. "What are you talking about, Ms. Barnes?"

Fran pursed her lips. "It's not Ms. Barnes. It's Mrs. Handel."

"Mrs. Handel?" Judge Caldwell crossed his arms. "You mean to tell the court that you're married to Nicholas Handel?"

Dane felt his insides churn. Fran had played them. He didn't know how or why, but somehow his father's assistant was about to ruin their lives. His balled up his hands, and in his anger he ignored the pain shooting through his hands.

"Yes," Fran replied. "I can show you our marriage license if you'd like."

An audible gasp rippled through the courtroom and Judge Caldwell banged his gavel. "Order! Can the prosecution and the defense approach the bench?"

Lester quickly headed over to the judge, a bewildered expression on his face.

Allyson turned in her seat, her eyes searching. When their eyes met, Dane saw them widen with fear. This had completely blindsided her. The same way it had blindsided everyone else. If Fran really was married to Nicholas Handel, there was no way she could testify against her own husband. Dane was no lawyer, but he knew enough to know about spousal privileges. If Fran couldn't back up his father's testimony they were sunk, and Allyson would go back to jail.

Fran was Nicholas' secret wife?

They were screwed. Royally.

Chapter 17

"This is a complete disaster," Lester said.

Allyson forced air into her lungs. She was in a never-ending nightmare. If her own lawyer thought she was in trouble, there was no fixing this. In the short amount of time she had known Lester, she had never seen him agitated. Now he was pacing up and down the office, his hands balled up so tight his knuckles were white.

Her husband was leaning against the closed door, his jaw clenched.

They were in Judge Caldwell's office. The judge had given them a chance to talk over strategy now that Francesca Barnes...*Handel* had dropped a bombshell.

It was some kind of cruel irony to find out about Nicholas Handel's secret marriage after she and Dane had themselves married in secret.

A knock on the office door nearly made her jump out of her chair.

Dane stepped aside to open the door. Francesca sashayed in, a smile on her face.

More like a smirk.

Allyson narrowed her eyes. "What are you doing here?"

"I've come to tender my resignation," Fran purred, shutting the door behind her.

"I suspect Alfred will want you fired anyway," Allyson said tersely.

Fran crossed her arms, her eyes sweeping over the room as if she owned the place. "That was always your problem, Allyson. You are such an entitled—"

"Watch what you say next," Dane interrupted.

Fran laughed. "I've been dreaming of this moment for months. You're not going to ruin it for me, Dane dear."

"You framed me." Allyson couldn't keep the accusation out of her voice.

"Of course I framed you," Fran said with a sneer. "New York and the entire East Coast society have been gunning for you ever since that first photo of you in that wedding dress made the papers. You're a usurper. You don't belong here."

"Is that why you did this?" Lester demanded. "Was all of this some petty stunt because my client isn't the right sort of person?"

Fran crossed the office and sat down at the judge's desk. She raised her chin, a look of triumph on her face. "This is me fixing things. Making sure the natural order gets restored. People like me don't end up taking orders from the likes of you, Allyson."

A chill crept down Allyson's spine. Lester was wrong. This wasn't petty. There was a hatred burning in Francesca's eyes. "What is this? Did you marry Nicholas to get back at me or something?"

"I love Nicholas," Fran snapped. "We met a year ago. We fell in love. But we couldn't be together because I wasn't good enough for his mother and his sister. My family used to be important. Until my stupid brother fell in love with a social-climbing, gold-digging tramp who reminds me so much of you, Allyson. And then that gold-digger ruined us and left my entire family broke. That's why I have to do menial jobs to make ends meet. I've been acting like a damn servant for months."

Realization dawned on Allyson. It was too late now, but the puzzle pieces were finally falling into place. "You married Nicholas Handel in secret because his family wouldn't accept you."

"But they accepted you," Fran bit out, her voice dripping with venom. "Sure, everyone hated you. They still let you in to high society anyway after you married Dane and saved Prescott. You got invited to the most exclusive parties. Made friends with people who ordinarily wouldn't give you the time of day. Somehow, you've managed to keep on climbing, Allyson. You were a nobody. From a nothing family, with no money and no breeding. You were just an assistant, for bloody sake." Fran's face turned crimson, her entire body shaking with unrestrained fury.

"So you framed me to get rid of me?"

"Yes. I also needed the money so that Nicky's family would finally accept me. Embezzling funds from Prescott was just killing two birds with one stone. I'd get rid of you once and for all, and I'd finally have enough money to buy my way back into the upper class." Fran smoothed her hair, her rage seeming to melt away now.

Allyson glared. "So you hate me because I'm from a middle-class family."

"I hate you because you're living my life. Your husband parades you around like he's proud of you. Like he doesn't care that you're a cheap, low-class tramp everyone secretly hates and envies. Somehow you got this fancy job and this perfect life," Fran said. "I hated you enough to work with that cow, Katherine. She knew how I felt about Nicky, but she kept reminding me that I wasn't good enough for her family. Still, I teamed up with her because I thought if I helped break up you and Dane, she'd accept me. Let me be with Nicholas."

"Let me guess," Dane said. "Katherine Handel knifed you in the back."

"She swore she'd get me a good job. Swore she'd talk me up to her family so that they'd let me be with Nicky. But after you chased her and Nicky back to England, she totally screwed me over," Fran said. "There was no fancy job. Katherine just used me to try to destroy you, Allyson. When that didn't work, she left me high and dry. Joke's on her, though. I married Nicky."

"She has no idea," Allyson pointed out.

"She will soon," Fran said icily. "Then she'll realize that she lost. She lost Dane to you. And she'll lose Nicky to me. I'll be the most important woman in the Handel family. Not her."

Allyson stared in stunned silence. The loathing that seemed to consume Francesca was palpable. For months she had believed that Katherine Handel had been her most dangerous enemy, but seeing Fran now in her hideous glory, Allyson realized the truth. Katherine might have been ruthless, but Francesca Barnes would kill to get what she wanted. "You sent the attacker after me, didn't you?" she choked out. "That night outside the hotel. You sent someone to hit me with a baseball bat."

Fran laughed. "I didn't send anyone. *I'm* the one who hit you with the bat. A pair of boots and a mask make a perfect disguise in the dark. You were an idiot to not realize it was a woman."

"You're lucky you're a woman," Dane growled.

"Yes, I know how chivalrous you are, Dane," Fran mocked. "So honorable. So noble. You hit poor Nicky, but I know you'd never lay a finger on me no matter how badly I beat your wife."

"Nicholas doesn't know what you've done, does he?" Allyson asked suddenly, the realization dawning on her.

Fran shook her head. "Nope. If he did he'd probably never forgive me. Which is why you have to go away for a long time dear, sweet Allyson."

"How did you do all of this?" Allyson tried to think back to all the moments where she might have worked out what Fran was up to. She wracked her brain, trying to figure out what she hadn't been able to see.

"Easy. After Nicky and I got married I got a job as an assistant at Prescott. Then, I started funneling money out of Prescott's New York accounts to an account in London," Fran replied. "Framing you was the easiest thing in the world. I made sure to funnel money through the women's division, so you'd be the prime suspect. After that, it was so easy to slip some damning information into the box of files I handed over to Detective Rossi."

Allyson's heart sank at the realization. Fran really had been that devious and calculating. That cunning. "Oh my goodness..."

"No one's going to save you now," Fran said, smirking.

"You sent that threatening note," Allyson said.

Fran nodded. "I was the last one to leave your room that day. Dropping the note was easy. I needed you out of London. I needed you to stop snooping around. I couldn't have you figuring things out before the cops were ready to put you back in jail. But you didn't leave."

"No," Allyson said evenly. "I didn't leave. It takes more than a note to scare me off."

"I figured that," Fran snapped. "Then I saw you sneak into Nicky's office at his flat, and I suspected you discovered something important. You left me no choice. I had to scare you into leaving London *and* get back whatever it was that you had stolen from Nicky."

"You knew the will was in my handbag?" Allyson asked.

"No, I just guessed," Fran replied. "It's a good thing you left London when you did, Allyson. Especially now that you'll be put on trial. You'll be put away for years."

"Why would you do this?" Allyson demanded. "I'm not a threat to you. I didn't keep you from marrying Nicholas. I didn't take your family's money."

"You're living a life you don't deserve," Fran said. "And you hurt Nicky. After he took control of Prescott Global six months ago, you drove him out. You almost ruined his reputation. Then you had the nerve to attack him, Dane. You just can't leave Nicky alone, can you?"

"So all this is revenge," Allyson said.

"You don't get to judge me," Fran said shrilly. "You do what you have to do for your husband. I'm doing what I have to do for mine."

As crazy as it sounded, Allyson could understand what Fran meant. The woman was cruel and horrible, but in her twisted, vindictive mind she had stolen and assaulted to keep and protect the man she loved. Allyson knew how it felt to risk everything for love. She had been willing to face jail time to save Dane from his own reckless, protective instincts. "How long have you been planning all this anyway?"

"Well, since the merger with Handel and Company," Fran replied. "I had already met Nicky, but Katherine forced us to break up. You weren't in the picture then, so I hadn't been planning on ruining you, Allyson. But I did plan on getting my hands on enough money to force the Handels to accept me. The merger seemed as good a time as any to make my move and get into Prescott Global so that I could get some money. Only, you kept getting in the way. First, Katherine made me tell her every bit of gossip I heard about you. And then you tried to ruin Nicky."

"You're not getting away with this," Dane said forcefully.

"Wake up, Dane," Fran said. "The judge has you in here because this is exactly where he wants you. Without my testimony to back up your father's claims, the charges against Allyson won't be dropped. Which means she'll be back in police custody before the day is over. Even if for some reason she's eventually found innocent she'll still spend months if not years in jail, waiting for the trial. By that time your marriage will probably be destroyed, and you'll be nothing more than a memory, Allyson."

"And you'll be back on top," Allyson said coldly.

"You flew too close to the sun," Fran said with a shrug. "It happens."

"You've just confessed everything to us," Lester said. "We can go to the judge with this."

"With what evidence?" Fran got to her feet. "You think you're the first person to go to the judge with a story about being framed?" She laughed. "Get real. Without evidence, you have nothing. No proof. No case against me."

Without another word, Francesca Handel sauntered out of the office.

The silence in the room was almost maddening. Dane was glaring at the door. Lester's shoulders were slumped in defeat. All Allyson wanted to do was scream and cry. She was completely and utterly out of her depth. Her feud with Katherine looked like a minor tiff compared to this. Prison. She might actually end up spending years in prison.

The awful horror of it all washed over her.

She didn't have time to catch her breath before the door swung open again. Two police officers stood in the doorway, one holding a pair of handcuffs.

The urge to run was impossible to ignore. She was trapped and there was no escape.

Dane advanced towards the officers, shielding her with his body. "You stay the hell away from my wife."

Judge Caldwell appeared. "We don't want to do this, but you don't have enough witnesses or any compelling evidence. After the so-called attack in London you've given me no choice but to put you back into custody, Mrs. Prescott."

"But the attack was real," she cried desperately. "Someone did attack me. Francesca Barnes attacked me."

"Enough!" Judge Caldwell glowered at her. "Take her into custody immediately."

The two officers forced their way past Dane and grabbed her arms. The thought of being put back into a jail cell terrified her so much she wanted to scream. But this time, as one of the officers handcuffed her, she didn't put up a fight. Didn't even say a word. Because she knew it was no use.

Chapter 18

There would never be a worse moment than this. Nothing could ever compare to watching the police haul his wife away for the second time. Except, this time she didn't struggle. Didn't call out to him. As they dragged her out of the office, she didn't even meet his gaze.

Dane chased after them. Shouted threats at the officers. But they shoved her into a police car and sped off, away from the courthouse. Lester was right on his heels as reporters closed in.

"Get in the car," Dane said harshly. "We're going back to the police station. We're getting her out."

"That isn't a good idea, Mr. Prescott," Lester said, his voice irritatingly calm.

"The hell it isn't!" Dane bit out. "They've just taken my wife, goddamn it. I'm going down to the station with or without you."

"If you make the police angry, they won't treat Mrs. Prescott very well," Lester warned. "Think about this. You want your wife to have as easy a time as possible in there. If you antagonize the police, they'll take it out on her."

A hot, desperate rage roiled through him. They had taken her from him. Just dragged her off like she had done something wrong, when in reality Allyson was the victim. That viper, Francesca, was responsible for this nightmare.

"So, what do we do?" Dane asked. "You can't expect me to accept this. To let her suffer in jail until a trial. And if you lose the case when it comes to trial..." His stomach tightened. There was a very real chance that he would never see Allyson ever again outside of a cell or a court-house.

Today might very well be the last day he would ever see her as a free woman. From now on she might always be behind bars, behind glass, or handcuffed.

No. He refused to accept that. Refused to give up on the only woman he would ever love. There was no life without Allyson. No point in living if she wasn't by his side.

Lester gestured for him to follow and they forced their way back into the courthouse, leaving the crowd of reporters behind.

Dane's phone started ringing. Yanking it out of his pocket to drop the call, he saw that it was from Katherine Handel. Why in the world was she calling him?

Rage made him answer the phone. He wanted to take his rage out on every Handel who had ever lived. The merger had been the worst business decision he had ever made. The more entwined the Prescotts became with the Handels, the worse his life got.

"What the hell do you want?" he growled.

"Is that any way to speak to an old friend?" Katherine chirped.

He swore loudly. "Now isn't a good time. I'm hanging up now."

"Oh, I don't think you want to do that, darling," she purred. "You're going to want to hear what I have to say."

THE DRIVE TO MANHATTAN was a long nightmare. Traffic almost made Dane want to punch through the windows of the car.

As the chauffer pulled up to the luxury apartment block, Dane stepped out of the car and rushed upstairs to the top floor. He had left Lester behind at the courthouse like Katherine Handel had requested. It didn't matter that he knew he was walking into a trap. Some petty, vindictive nonsense Katherine had cooked up. As long as there was a chance he could save his wife, he'd hear Katherine Handel out.

After ringing the doorbell, Martha Faraway opened the door and ushered him inside.

"Thank you for letting us use your apartment for this meeting," Dane said to Martha. Katherine had insisted on meeting somewhere private and away from potential tabloid reporters. He had texted Martha, hoping that there was a chance one of Allyson's friends might help, and Martha had been kind enough to offer to let him meet in her home.

Martha was a socialite who sometimes appeared in gossip rags, but a lot of that had died down since she had married Gordon Faraway, a self-made millionaire who had made his money in office supplies of all things. The Faraways' luxury apartment was as out of the way and private as they were going to get.

Martha smiled as they stepped into the living room. "Of course. Anything for Allyson."

He paused. Stared at Martha for a moment. Clearly, he had misjudged his wife's friends. Had been convinced they were disloyal and scheming like so many people in the upper class. But now, Martha and her husband had graciously let him into their home. Despite knowing that Allyson had been just been arrested again. "I really am grateful," he said finally.

Gordon Faraway was already in the living room, talking to Katherine Handel, who was sitting on a chair like it was a throne. Her blond hair cascaded down her back, her blue eyes as icy as ever.

"Hello, Dane." Gordon stood up and gave Dane a quick, firm handshake. "It's wonderful to see you again, in spite of the circumstances. I can't believe this is going to trial. It's absolute madness. Please let us know if there's anything we can do for you and Allyson."

"I will," Dane said. "Thank you, Gordon."

"We'll be more than happy to be character witnesses at the trial," Martha said. "It's the least we can do, considering how obvious it is that Allyson is innocent. She doesn't have a dishonest bone in her body."

"Other than her fake marriage fiasco," Katherine cut in.

"Didn't you have something to do with that, Katherine?" Martha flashed Katherine a smile that didn't reach her eyes.

Katherine sniffed. "If you could just give Dane and me a moment—"

"Oh, how rude of me," Martha said. "Gordon and I can give you two some privacy. Or, better yet, you can talk on the roof. It's very private up there."

After Gordon and Martha led them up to the roof of the apartment and left them alone, Dane regarded Katherine with suspicion.

Her lips curved up into a cruel smile. "I saw your poor wife getting dragged away in handcuffs on the news."

"You sound really cut up about it," he muttered. "What's all this about? You claim you know a way to help Allyson but you wanted to meet in secret, and you insisted I come here alone."

"It wasn't very nice of you to hit my brother."

He clenched his teeth. If she knew the truth, that he had wanted to do more than punch her brother, she probably wouldn't help him. And he needed that help. Even if it meant he couldn't tell Katherine that he wanted to beat her brother within an inch of his life when he had thought Nicholas had been the one who attacked Allyson. "Your brother's an ass. You know it as well as I do."

Katherine headed over to the edge of the roof and stared down. Turning to him, she beckoned.

Dane didn't trust her, but he didn't have much of a choice. Apprehension twisting his gut, he sauntered over to her. It was an unseasonably warm day, so at least there weren't going to freeze out here. "Get to the point."

She pouted. "You've always had atrocious manners. Unlike your wife, who has always been far more sociable. She doesn't have our breeding, but she certainly makes up for it with her charm and good manners."

"I don't have time for this." He pulled away from her, but her hand on his arm stopped him.

"I wouldn't be so quick to leave if I were you," she said. "I know a way to save your wife."

"Why would you want to help her?" he demanded. "You hate Allyson."

Her hand lifted to wrap a lock of her golden hair around her finger. "I do. But even I have to admit she has her strengths. I can admire a woman who beats me at my own game. I really underestimated her. First, she married you, and then she got Prescott Global back for you. I used to think she was the lucky one for marrying you, but now I'm not so sure."

"You thought she was the lucky one because you're an unrepentant snob," he said. "Anyone who wasn't obsessed with money could see I'm the lucky one in this marriage."

"Damn, you actually love her," Katherine said. "It's honestly nauseating. What is it with rich men and poor women? Nicky's the same way."

His body tensed. "You know about Nicky? And Francesca?"

"Do I know that they're married? Yes."

"How did you figure that out?" he asked, intrigued despite everything.

"I found Nicky's will," she said. "Right before she flew back to New York to testify, Fran had brought some of her things over to his place as some childish show that she had slept over at his flat. I think she wanted to show me that they were sleeping together. Weeks ago I had guessed that they were back together, but I didn't realize that they had been stupid enough to actually get married until I found the will."

He raised an eyebrow. "You flew out here from London just to tell me this?"

"The will is the evidence, darling." She rolled her eyes, as if it was the most obvious thing in the world.

"I don't follow."

"Simple. I have the evidence that can free your wife, and put Fran in jail for the rest of her miserable life," Katherine said.

Dane leaned forward and gave her a hard stare.

She laughed. "Do I have your attention now?"

"You do. Now make it worth my while, Katherine," he growled.

"Why should I help you?" She pouted, and he was almost tempted to punch her. Of course, he wouldn't. But the woman was so... frustrating at times.

He shoved aside his annoyance. She was obviously toying with him. Dangling something she had no intention of handing over freely. "You're the one who offered to help. Now you're asking me why you should follow through?"

"You're so tedious," she grumbled. "You were so much more fun before Allyson showed up and stole you away from me."

"I was never yours to begin with," he said coldly. "Clearly, you want something in exchange for your help. Fine. What do you want?"

Katherine's hand lifted again, and she wrapped his tie around her wrist. "If I help you get your wife out of jail, you have to help me in return."

"I'm not going to sleep with you," he said flatly. There was no way in hell he could ever be unfaithful to Allyson. He'd do anything to save his wife. Go to jail in her place. Even die if he had to. But he could never betray her by cheating.

"You think I'm going to go through all this trouble for one night of great sex?" She sneered. "It's like you don't even know me at all."

"So what do you want, then?" he demanded. What on earth could a woman who had everything possibly want? Katherine had wealth, beauty, power, fame, and access to the most eligible bachelors on earth. There was almost nothing she couldn't have.

"I want a promise," she replied. "I want you to promise to owe me a favor. And you have to swear that when I call in this favor, you'll deliver. You'll do whatever it is that I ask you."

"I'm not going to do anything violent or illegal," he muttered. "So if you expect me to do anything that harms another person—"

Her mocking laughter cut him off. "Don't worry, I'm not asking you to give up your first-born child. And you won't have to kill or assault anyone. All you have to do is swear to do as I ask, and Allyson will be a free woman."

Swearing to something like this was dangerous. There was no telling what Katherine would want him to do. Whatever it was that she eventually wanted would probably be unsavory at the very least. But he had to save Allyson. Even if the price was selling his soul to Katherine Handel. "I'll promise to owe you a favor," he said slowly. "But only if you can deliver on your end. The charges against Allyson actually have to be dropped."

"I have evidence that implicates Francesca in all of this," she said. "I found Allyson's handbag with Francesca's things. I recognized it because Allyson brought it with her on the day she toured Prescott's London offices."

"The handbag that Francesca stole from Allyson after she attacked her," he said. "What about the bat?"

"I don't have the bat." She shook her head. "But inside the purse was Nicky's will."

He frowned, still skeptical. "You think that's enough to implicate Fran?"

"Allyson's blood was on the bag," Katherine said. "I've spoken to my lawyer. She believes that's enough to prove that Francesca attacked Allyson to prevent the truth about her secret marriage to Nicky from getting out."

"And Nicholas having an heir means there's proof the embezzled funds went into the heir's trust," he said, realization dawning on him.

"Exactly."

"Why are you helping me?" he pressed. "What's in it for you?"

"I'm not helping you. I'm helping me," she answered. "The only person I hate more than Allyson is that witch, Francesca. She got her hooks into Nicholas, and I know she's scheming to get her grubby little hands on our family's fortune. So if I can destroy Francesca and get you to owe me a favor at the same time, that's what I'm going to do."

"Fran seems to have the impression that you're the one who knifed her in the back." He glanced at her meaningfully. "You have a habit of doing that."

"It's called business, darling. It's nothing personal," she said with a smile.

He narrowed his eyes. "All I know is this had better work. Because if you're messing with me, or lying, I'm going to spend the rest of my life making yours a waking nightmare."

The smile on her face disappeared. "I already know the price of crossing you. I'll deliver. Just make sure that when I call in my favor you do exactly as I ask. Don't be fooled by your momentary triumph over me. Because the only thing worse than crossing a Prescott is crossing a Handel."

Chapter 19

The reporters at the police station were in a frenzy.

As Dane stepped out of the car, they shoved their cameras and microphones in his face. Ignoring them, he marched into the station. He had to see her. Had to make sure that this had worked.

When he walked inside the station he stopped by Allyson, standing beside Lester and a couple of police officers. His wife had been in jail overnight while Katherine had gone to the police with her evidence.

He hadn't slept at all last night. Mostly he spent the night downing scotch and calling Lester to make sure he was working on getting Allyson's charges dropped. Then late this morning, Lester had called to let him know that Allyson was getting out after the charges were dropped. Charges against Francesca had been filed.

Allyson looked so fragile. There were dark circles under her eyes, her face was pale. When her eyes met his a smile lit her face, her exhausted expression disappearing. She was practically glowing, she was so beautiful.

Dane rushed over, quickly thanked Lester, and then pulled Allyson into his arms. He didn't give a damn about protocol. All he wanted to do was hold her in his arms and never let her go.

"I love you," she said before pressing her soft lips to his. Crushing her mouth beneath his, he tasted her. Teased her mouth open with his tongue. There had been a moment last night when he wondered if he would ever kiss his wife again. And now that he could, he knew that nothing would ever taste sweeter.

Breaking the kiss, she stared deep into his eyes and asked, "How did you do this? How did you save me?"

He hesitated. The expectant look in her green eyes knocked the wind out of him. She was gazing at him with complete reverence and adoration. Like she thought he was some savior for getting her out of jail.

If she knew that he was in Katherine Handel's debt, her happiness would melt away. After the hell Francesca had put her through, she deserved to be happy. Besides, if he could pay Katherine back in secret, Allyson never had to find out about his deal and she would never have to worry. He'd simply sign on to stay on as Prescott Global's CEO for the foreseeable future to protect the company from Katherine, and nobody would have to know why he was staying on.

"It was all Lester," he replied.

"Lester did so much, but I don't believe it was all him," she whispered. "Your parents know Judge Caldwell, don't they? I bet you pulled a few strings—"

"I should've killed you with that baseball bat when I had the chance, you bitch!" Francesca's screech filled the police station.

Cops were dragging her into the station. Her face was red with rage, and she struggled violently against the police who were shoving her forward.

Allyson held on even tighter to him, her lower lip quivering. "I know she's horrible, but I understand what she's about to go through. In a way."

"I should have finished you off!" Fran lunged at Allyson, but the cops restrained her. "Next time you won't be so lucky!"

They police pulled her out of sight, Fran's angry shrieks getting fainter and fainter.

"I figured out what Nicholas sees in her," Allyson said.

"What?"

"She's exactly like his sister," she said. "I know Fran hates Katherine, but it's scary how alike they are."

After witnessing Katherine's dark, devious nature up close on the rooftop yesterday, he knew that she and Fran really were two halves of the same tarnished coin. If Katherine had been willing to destroy her own brother's happiness for her own gain, she wouldn't hesitate to crush him if he didn't deliver on his promise. Owing Katherine Handel was a nightmare scenario.

He ignored the tightening in his chest. None of that mattered now. Allyson was free. They could start the next chapter of their lives together.

Taking her chin in her hands, he stared at her. Really took her in. His gaze swept over every line and arch of her face. Drank in her bright green eyes and her perfect mouth. She was so beautiful his heart ached at the sight of her. "I love you, Allyson."

"And I love you," she said. "My hero."

Pushing aside the guilt he felt about keeping the truth from her, Dane offered her his arm and she took it. "Why don't we get you out of here?"

"And then we can get back to us," she said.

Together they headed out of the station. "What would you like to do now that you're a free woman?" he asked.

She smiled. "I think it's time we moved in to our new house."

"YOU CHOSE THE PERFECT color." She turned away from the blue wall to look at Dane, and let out a laugh. "You've got paint on your face. It matches your eyes."

He grinned. "You've got some on your nose."

Allyson giggled. "Who knew wall painting could be so much fun?" With the roller in her hands, she applied more blue paint to the wall of their home office.

Updates on their new house had been coming along nicely in the two weeks since she'd gotten out of jail. Working on renovations was tiring, but in a good way. It was wonderful to get back to doing normal things instead of worrying about going to jail. As long as she lived, she would never take her freedom for granted ever again. Even something as mundane as painting the house with Dane was a treasure for her.

"You know, when we have kids they'll probably ruin these walls," he said. "I remember drawing all over the walls of our homes with markers and crayons when I was a kid. That was a nightmare for my mother. And it drove the maids crazy." He smiled. "I can't wait to work in here while our kids are growing up."

"It'll be wonderful to be able to work from home and be close to them," she said.

"I'm just happy you're here," he said, his voice thick with emotion.

She tilted her head and looked at him. It wasn't like him to show his emotions like this. "I'm happy to be here. Thank you for saving me."

"No thanks needed." He quickly averted his gaze to focus on painting more of the wall.

The past two weeks had been such a happy blur that she hadn't felt the nagging feeling that she felt now. Dane had renewed his contract to stay on at Prescott Global, despite his reservations. Plus, he had talked to her about plans he had beyond Prescott Global. He was interested in sports media or sports cars. It all sounded so exciting, but she couldn't help the uneasy sensation that was now making her stomach knot up.

"Is everything all right?" she asked.

"Absolutely," he said. "We'll have the place looking brand-new in no time. Then we can have that house-warming party you wanted."

She smiled. "I'm so happy you've decided to give Gordon and Martha a chance. What made you so eager to have them over?"

"They make you happy," he said. "And what makes you happy, makes me happy. Happy wife, happy life."

"Are you happy?" she asked. "I know staying on at Prescott Global wasn't easy, but I'll be here to help you with all your new ideas. Your sports car idea sounds incredible."

"Are you still going to be saying that if I actually buy a sports car?" he asked.

"Do I get to ride up front with you?"

"I wouldn't have anybody else up front with me," he replied.

Her smile widened. "Then I promise to love your car."

They returned their attention to painting the walls.

"You know," Dane said after a stretch of comfortable silence, "I'm not one for decorating, but I can't wait to get my hands on a grill."

She gave him an incredulous look. In their more than six months of marriage, he hadn't learned enough to do more than boil an egg. "Dane Prescott can grill?"

He chuckled. "I can learn."

"I think we'll be learning all kinds of new things in this house," she said.

"I don't think I've ever been this happy," he told her.

She paused, and turned to look at him. Before getting arrested, her happiness had terrified her. She had spent six months waiting for the other shoe to drop. The truth was, there was always a chance that things would go sideways again. Always a chance that there would be hardships ahead. But she wasn't going to be so afraid of her own happiness that she ran away from it. Not with Dane by her side.

He was her hero. Her protector. Her knight in shining armor. "Every day with you is happier than the day before," she said.

He dropped his roller and wrapped his strong arms around her.

"Dane, you're going to get paint all over my blouse!" she shrieked.

"How about we get you out of this blouse, then?" he asked in a low voice that was already seducing her.

Laughing she let go of her roller, flung her arms around him, and melted against him as he kissed her like she was the only woman in the world.

THE END

Faking It
Book 1
Temporary CEO
Book 2
Caught in the Act
Book 3
Never Tell a Lie
Book 4
Fake Christmas
Book 5 Novella

Fake Christmas Blurb:

"BETTER TO BE SLAPPED with the truth than hurt with a lie."

Dane Prescott has everything. He's a 35-year-old billionaire, owner and CEO of Prescott Enterprise, and married to the most gorgeous, sweetest woman in the world. He loves her even more than the day they got married. Lately though, this is a distance growing between the two of them and Dane is terrified Allyson might have had enough of high class society.

When a thunderstorm in New York forces them to change direction of their private jet, Dane hopes the unexpected Christmas weekend south will rekindle the hot-passion between them.

Except is Allyson keeping secrets from him?

Will their love be strong enough to survive the secrets she's been hiding?

More by Lexy Timms:

FROM BEST SELLING AUTHOR, Lexy Timms, comes a billionaire romance that'll make you swoon and fall in love all over again.

Jamie Connors has given up on men. Despite being smart, pretty, and just slightly overweight, she's a magnet for the kind of guys that don't stay around.

Her sister's wedding is at the foreground of the family's attention. Jamie would be find with it if her sister wasn't pressuring her to lose weight so she'll fit in the maid of honor dress, her mother would get off her case and her ex-boyfriend wasn't about to become her brother-in-law.

Determined to step out on her own, she accepts a PA position from billionaire Alex Reid. The job includes an apartment on his property and gets her out of living in her parent's basement.

JAMIE HAS TO BALANCE her life and somehow figure out how to manage her billionaire boss, without falling in love with him.

** The Boss is book 1 in the Managing the Bosses series. All your questions won't be answered in the first book. It may end on a cliff hanger.

For mature audiences only. There are adult situations, but this is a love story, NOT erotica.

Capturing Her Beauty

KAYLA REID HAS ALWAYS been into fashion and everything to do with it. Growing up wasn't easy for her. A bigger girl trying to squeeze into the fashion world is like trying to suck an entire gelatin mold through a straw; possible, but difficult.

She found herself an open door as a designer and jumped right in. Her designs always made the models smile. The colors, the fabrics, the styles. Never once did she dream of being on the other side of the lens. She got to watch her clothing strut around on others and that was good enough.

But who says you can't have a little fun when you're off the clock?

Sometimes trying on the latest fashions is just as good as making them. Kayla's hours in front of the mirror were a guilty pleasure.

A chance meeting with one of the company photographers may turn into more than just an impromptu photo shoot.

Hot n' Handsome, Rich & Single... how far are you willing to go?
MEET ALEX REID, CEO of Reid Enterprise. Billionaire extra ordinaire, chiseled to perfection, panty-melter and currently single.

Learn about Alex Reid before he began Managing the Bosses. Alex Reid sits down for an interview with R&S.

His life style is like his handsome looks: hard, fast, breath-taking and out to play ball. He's risky, charming and determined.

How close to the edge is Alex willing to go? Will he stop at nothing to get what he wants?

Alex Reid is book 1 in the R&S Rich and Single Series. Fall in love with these hot and steamy men; all single, successful, and searching for love.

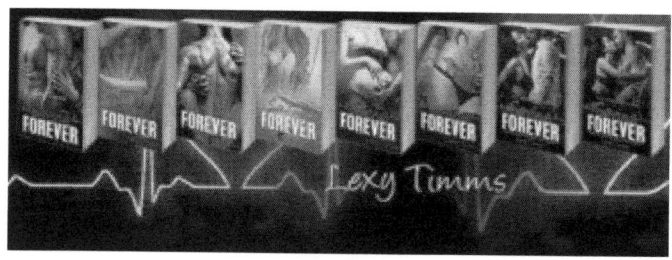

Sometimes the heart needs a different kind of saving... find out if Charity Thompson will find a way of saving forever in this hospital setting Best-Selling Romance by Lexy Timms

Charity Thompson wants to save the world, one hospital at a time. Instead of finishing med school to become a doctor, she chooses a different path and raises money for hospitals – new wings, equipment, whatever they need. Except there is one hospital she would be happy to never set foot in again—her fathers. So of course he hires her to create a gala for his sixty-fifth birthday. Charity can't say no. Now she is working in the one place she doesn't want to be. Except she's attracted to Dr. Elijah Bennet, the handsome playboy chief.

Will she ever prove to her father that's she's more than a med school dropout? Or will her attraction to Elijah keep her from repairing the one thing she desperately wants to fix?

Heart of the Battle Series
In a world plagued with darkness, she would be his salvation.
No one gave Erik a choice as to whether he would fight or not. Duty to the crown belonged to him, his father's legacy remaining beyond the grave.

Taken by the beauty of the countryside surrounding her, Linzi would do anything to protect her father's land. Britain is under attack and Scotland is next. At a time she should be focused on suitors, the men of her country have gone to war and she's left to stand alone.

Love will become available, but will passion at the touch of the enemy unravel her strong hold first?

THE RECRUITING TRIP

Aspiring college athlete Aileen Nessa is finding the recruiting process beyond daunting. Being ranked #10 in the world for the 100m hurdles at the age of eighteen is not a fluke, even though she believes that one race, where everything clinked magically together, might be. American universities don't seem to think so. Letters are pouring in from all over the country.

As she faces the challenge of differentiating between a college's genuine commitment to her or just empty promises from talent-seeking coaches, Aileen heads to the University of Gatica, a Division One school, on a recruiting trip. Her best friend dares who to go just to see the cute guys on the school's brochure.

The university's athletic program boasts one of the top hurdlers in the country. Tyler Jensen is the school's NCAA champion in the hurdles and Jim Thorpe recipient for top defensive back in football. His incredible blue-green eyes, confident smile and rock hard six pack abs mess with Aileen's concentration.

His offer to take her under his wing, should she choose to come to Gatica, is a temping proposition that has her wondering if she might be with an angel or making a deal with the devil himself.

THE ONE YOU CAN'T FORGET

Emily Rose Dougherty is a good Catholic girl from mythical Walkerville, CT. She had somehow managed to get herself into a heap trouble with the law, all because an ex-boyfriend has decided to make things difficult.

Luke "Spade" Wade owns a Motorcycle repair shop and is the Road Captain for Hades' Spawn MC. He's shocked when he reads in the paper that his old high school flame has been arrested. She's always been the one he couldn't forget.

Will destiny let them find each other again? Or what happens in the past, best left for the history books?

** *This is book 1 of the Hades' Spawn MC Series. All your questions may not be answered in the first book.*

And so much more to come!!

NOTE FROM LEXY:

THANKS FOR READING (and finding this last page note)

?

I just want to let you know that I always try and make the first books of my series free for readers. It gives you a chance to see if you like the storyline, enjoy characters and the setting. So check out my other stories and see if something gets your heart spinning!

Find Lexy Timms:

Lexy Timms Newsletter:
    http://eepurl.com/9i0vD
Lexy Timms Facebook Page:
https://www.facebook.com/SavingForever
Lexy Timms Website:
http://lexytimms.com
Lexy Timms Amazon Page:
http://www.amazon.com/Lexy-Timms/e/B00HZ3O3QW

Don't miss out!

Click the button below and you can sign up to receive emails whenever Lexy Timms publishes a new book. There's no charge and no obligation.

https://books2read.com/r/B-A-NNL-YGEP

BOOKS 2 READ

Connecting independent readers to independent writers.

Did you love *Never Tell A Lie*? Then you should read *Fragile Touch* by Lexy Timms!

USA Today Bestselling Author, Lexy Timms delivers a tender story of how the heart finds love in the most unexpected places.

"His body is perfect. He's got this face that isn't just heart-melting but actually kind of exotic..."

Lillian Warren's life is just how she's designed it. She has a high-paying job working with celebrities and the elite, teaching them how to better organize their lives. She's on her own, the days quiet, but she likes it that way. Especially since she's still figuring out how to live with her recent diagnosis of Crohn's disease. Her cats keep her company, and she's not the least bit lonely.

Fun-loving personal trainer, Cayden, thinks his neighbor is a killjoy. He's only seen her a few times, and the woman looks like she needs a drink or three. He knows how to party and decides to invite her to over—if he can find her. What better way to impress her than take care of her overgrown yard? She proceeds to thank him by throwing up in his painstakingly-trimmed-to-perfection bushes.

Something about the fragile, mysterious woman captivates him.

Something about this rough-on-the-outside bear of a man attracts Lily, despite her heart warning her to tread carefully.

Fragile Series:
Fragile Touch
Fragile Kiss
Fragile Love

Also by Lexy Timms

A Chance at Forever Series
Forever Perfect
Forever Desired
Forever Together

Alpha Bad Boy Motorcycle Club Triology
Alpha Biker
Alpha Revenge
Alpha Outlaw
Alpha Purpose

BBW Romance Series
Capturing Her Beauty
Pursuing Her Dreams
Tracing Her Curves

Beating the Biker Series
Making Her His

Making the Break

Conquering Warrior Series
Ruthless

Diamond in the Rough Anthology
Billionaire Rock
Billionaire Rock - part 2

Dominating PA Series
Her Personal Assistant - Part 1
Her Personal Assistant Box Set

Fake Billionaire Series
Faking It
Temporary CEO
Caught in the Act
Never Tell A Lie

Firehouse Romance Series
Caught in Flames
Burning With Desire
Craving the Heat
Firehouse Romance Complete Collection

Celtic Rune
Celtic Mann
Heart of the Battle Series Box Set

Just About Series
About Love

Justice Series
Seeking Justice
Finding Justice
Chasing Justice
Pursuing Justice
Justice - Complete Series

Love You Series
Love Life
Need Love
My Love

Managing the Bosses Series
The Boss
The Boss Too
Who's the Boss Now
Love the Boss
I Do the Boss
Wife to the Boss

Employed by the Boss
Brother to the Boss
Senior Advisor to the Boss
Forever the Boss
Gift for the Boss - Novella 3.5
Christmas With the Boss

Moment in Time
Highlander's Bride
Victorian Bride
Modern Day Bride
A Royal Bride
Forever the Bride

Outside the Octagon
Submit

RIP Series
Track the Ripper
Hunt the Ripper
Pursue the Ripper

R&S Rich and Single Series
Alex Reid
Parker

Saving Forever
Saving Forever - Part 1
Saving Forever - Part 2
Saving Forever - Part 3
Saving Forever - Part 4
Saving Forever - Part 5
Saving Forever - Part 6
Saving Forever Part 7
Saving Forever - Part 8
Saving Forever Boxset Books #1-3

Southern Romance Series
Little Love Affair
Siege of the Heart
Freedom Forever
Soldier's Fortune

Tattooist Series
Confession of a Tattooist
Surrender of a Tattooist
Heart of a Tattooist
Hopes & Dreams of a Tattooist

Tennessee Romance
Whisky Lullaby
Whisky Melody

Whisky Harmony

The Debt
The Debt: Part 1 - Damn Horse
The Debt: Complete Collection

The University of Gatica Series
The Recruiting Trip
Faster
Higher
Stronger
Dominate
No Rush
University of Gatica - The Complete Series

T.N.T. Series
Troubled Nate Thomas - Part 1
Troubled Nate Thomas - Part 2
Troubled Nate Thomas - Part 3

Undercover Series
Perfect For Me
Perfect For You
Perfect For Us

Unknown Identity Series
Unknown
Unpublished
Unexposed
Unsure

Unlucky Series
Unlucky in Love

Standalone
Wash
Loving Charity
Summer Lovin'
Christmas Magic: A Romance Anthology
Love & College
Billionaire Heart
First Love
Frisky and Fun Romance Box Collection
Managing the Bosses Box Set #1-3

Printed in Great Britain
by Amazon

61823601R00118